T0082752

My Sister's Tortillas

My Sister's Tortillas

Silvia Ibarra

MY SISTER'S TORTILLAS

Copyright © 2020 Silvia Ibarra.

All rights reserved. No part of this book may be used or reproduced by any means, graphic, electronic, or mechanical, including photocopying, recording, taping or by any information storage retrieval system without the written permission of the author except in the case of brief quotations embodied in critical articles and reviews.

Certain characters in this work are historical figures, and certain events portrayed did take place. However, this is a work of fiction. All of the other characters, names, and events as well as all places, incidents, organizations, and dialogue in this novel are either the products of the author's imagination or are used fictitiously.

iUniverse books may be ordered through booksellers or by contacting:

iUniverse
1663 Liberty Drive
Bloomington, IN 47403
www.iuniverse.com
844-349-9409

Because of the dynamic nature of the Internet, any web addresses or links contained in this book may have changed since publication and may no longer be valid. The views expressed in this work are solely those of the author and do not necessarily reflect the views of the publisher, and the publisher hereby disclaims any responsibility for them.

Any people depicted in stock imagery provided by Getty Images are models, and such images are being used for illustrative purposes only. Certain stock imagery © Getty Images.

ISBN: 978-1-6632-0533-9 (sc)
ISBN: 978-1-6632-0532-2 (e)

Library of Congress Control Number: 2020913065

Print information available on the last page.

iUniverse rev. date: 08/03/2020

To Rosario and Laura

Contents

Chapter 1

My family left in the middle of the night. We were traveling by wagon on a very desolate road just outside Tarandacuao, Guanajuato, right in the middle of Mexico. It was raining, and the mud was beginning to make our journey difficult.

California was our destination. Gold would be our prize for reaching the river in the forest. We would be gone for several weeks and then return home with plenty to share with our families.

I traveled with my mother, Florecita, my father, Baldomero, my brother, Jose, my aunt, Belen, her husband, Daniel, and their three children: Elida, Elena, and Francisco.

"Are we going to stop soon?" Mama asked, after a few hours on the road.

"We have a bit to go, so it's best to think of the road as your home ... for now," Papa said.

"I wonder how many people have gone down this road looking for their dreams like we are?" Mama asked as she held me in her arms, giving me milk from her body.

"Who knows? I hear that there's so much gold you can actually look into the river and see it sparkling. I always wondered what it would be like to travel this road. I'd watch the ranchers leave town, and I knew that one day, I too would travel across the border, to the new frontier," he said.

"Did you know there would be this much mud?" Mama asked.

The other wagon carried my mother's sister and her family. We could see my aunt Belen going back and forth in the back of the wagon, arranging things or playing games with her three children.

"We should stop here," Papa said.

"I'm not tired, if you want to keep going," Mama said.

"No, this is a good spot: close to the water and not too late to make camp. What's for dinner?" he asked.

"We have some meat leftover from last night and beans, of course," Mama said.

"Let's have the meat," he said.

"Good idea. It'll go bad if we don't eat it soon," Mama said.

We stopped by the river, and Papa and Daniel set up the beds on a grassy area between the wagons.

Mama tied me to herself, and she helped Belen spread the blankets on the floor for others to sleep.

While Belen and Papa cleaned up, we went to sleep with the other children.

"Papa, can you believe we've already come this far?" Belen asked.

"It's God's will that we have survived. I have to admit, I miss the quiet pace of our life in Tarandacuao, but we'll soon be rich!" Papa said.

"You sound so sure, Baldo. I hate traveling. I hope this is all worth it," said Belen.

"Trust me. Daniel and I have seen others come back with gold. He's doing this for you and your family," Papa said.

"Daniel is a good man. I married one of the best— one of the two best men in our village," said Belen.

"And I married the woman of my dreams," Papa said.

"You're lucky to have each other," she said.

She looked up at Papa as she cleaned the pots at the edge of the river.

"Your hem is getting wet, Belen. Maybe I should wash the pots, and you can finish by the fire," Papa said.

"No, I'm fine. I like getting my feet wet. I might bathe tomorrow while you and Daniel go hunting," she said.

"I hope we catch something," Papa said.

"Florecita needs to eat meat. She's been feeding the baby day and night," said Belen.

"That baby was a gift from God. I'm sure we made the right choice, even though traveling with a baby can be difficult," Papa said.

"There you are," Daniel said, coming from the camp.

"My love, did you set up our bed?" asked Belen.

"Yes. Look at her, Baldo. Isn't she an angel in this moonlight?" asked Daniel.

"Whatever you say." Papa looked away as Daniel kissed Belen. "I'll go check on the children and Florecita."

He left the teenagers by the water, to kiss under the moonlight.

"*Buenas noches.*" Papa pushed back the sheets between the wagons, which acted as walls between us and the older children. "Is everyone asleep?"

"Yes, don't make a sound. It took me forever to get Belen's girls to sleep. All they do is talk," Mama said, holding me in her arms.

"We hunt tomorrow," Papa said.

"Will we be safe without you?" Mama asked.

"The animals stay away from people. It's the food they want. So, make sure you put everything away." Papa put his arms around his wife. "I would never let anything happen to you, my love. You are everything to me."

"I wish we had brought more food that didn't need to be killed," Mama said.

"Don't worry about that. Just take care of yourself and the children, especially Rosa. Let me look at her before I go to sleep," Papa said, holding me in his arms.

"She'll wake up soon for another feeding, and I don't want her to cry and wake the other children. Where is Belen? She needs to help me more," Mama said.

"She and Daniel are kissing in the moonlight. This beautiful moon makes for a very romantic place, don't you think?" Papa asked, leaning in to kiss Mama.

"One kiss—I need to feed the baby." Mama kissed him quickly and then began to feed me once more.

"Good night, sweetheart," Papa said.

"Good night, my darling" She held his face and kissed him once more.

Mama held me close to her warm body and sang a sweet song as we all fell asleep. "Little trees, little trees under your shade, I hope to sleep until I fade."

When morning came, Papa came to let us know he was going to hunt. "It's almost time to go."

"Yes. Let me feed her once more, and then I'll get breakfast started," Mama said.

"I'll start the fire," Papa said, kissing Mama on the cheek.

"Good morning, Florecita," said Belen.

"Hello, Belen. Where were you last night? These are your kids too, you know?"

"I was with Daniel. Did you and the little one sleep well last night?" asked Belen.

"We did. She only woke up three times. I think she should be sleeping through the night very soon," Mama said.

"That's how it was with Elida. She was a good sleeper after the first few weeks. The hard part was feeding her real food. She threw it all over the place." Belen laughed.

Mama continued to feed me.

"So how are you and Baldo? This desert air makes me crazy for Daniel," said Belen.

"We're fine," Mama said.

"I'm just saying … I noticed you haven't been as affectionate as you always were," said Belen.

"Well, maybe when the baby sleeps through the night, I won't be so tired all the time," Mama said.

"Of course—you two will be at it in no time," said Belen.

"That's none of your business," Mama said.

"Don't worry; he's not going to notice that you put on a little weight. That's natural after having a baby," said Belen.

"He loves me, no matter what," Mama said.

"Of course; no need to feel insecure," Belen said as she hugged her sister.

Chapter 2

We'd been traveling for several weeks. The red-orange sunsets were spectacular, and I enjoyed sitting in Mama's lap while the wagon swayed from side to side.

Back in Mexico, there were villages where we could stop and rest. But here in Texas, the roads were lonely and cut through vast plains and desert.

Sometimes we'd hear coyotes howling through the night, singing their mating call. Every now and then, we would swim in a beautiful river near the hills. I would sit on Papa's lap while the river ran over my knees.

At night, Papa and Daniel would light a fire and tell spooky stories.

Daniel said, "The bird-witches would fall down from their branches when people prayed the rosary below them. This made them turn into women! Afterward, they'd get up and run into the darkness."

"Have you heard the one about La Llorona," Papa asked.

The children huddled together to listen to the next story.

"Once upon a time, there was a woman who drowned her children in the ocean and cried for them every night, slowly going crazy. It is said that every time one hears the wind whistle through a crack in the window, you could hear her say, 'My children! Where are my children?'"

Daniel screamed from behind a tree, and everyone jumped in their seats. "Got you!" he said.

"Papa!" cried Elida.

"We weren't afraid," Jose said and Francisco.

"Well, I was!" said Elida.

"Baldo!" Mama said.

"Yes, my dear?"

"We're trying to sleep over here," she whispered. "Daniel, tell Belen to get the children to bed."

Daniel said, "Not sure where she is right now. I think she went to the river. I'll put the beds together for the little ones."

"We're not tired," said the boys.

"You knew we'd have to go to bed sometime. Tomorrow, we have to rise early to hunt for our supper. Now you boys go and get some water to put out the fire, and, Elida, you get the blankets spread out. Daniel, where is Belen?" Papa asked.

"I think she went to wash her clothes in the river. She couldn't have gone too far. You go over there, and I'll look that way," Daniel said.

Papa went close to the edge of the water. A few minutes later, he found her swimming in the river. "Belen?" He heard her singing but was unable to see her in the dark.

"Baldo!" she said.

"Sorry to disturb you, but Flora wanted to know if you could come help her," he said.

"Whatever! She wants me to take care of the children again? I'm tired of being a babysitter."

"Well, three of them are yours," Papa said.

"I know. Where is Daniel?" asked Belen.

"He's out looking for you," Papa said.

The moonlight moved from behind a cloud, giving a better view of Belen in the river.

"Isn't it beautiful out here?" she asked as she waded through the slow current.

"I suppose. Listen, I'll see you at the camp." Papa began walking away.

"I wonder if California is as beautiful as it is here," she added.

"Well, whether it is or isn't, gold is beautiful," Papa said.

"Don't you think this place is like Ojo de Dios?" said Belen.

"Ojo de Dios?"

"You know, with the streaming water and the trees all around. It reminds me of it," said Belen.

"It's similar in some ways. I bet you didn't know that Flor and I used to swim there at night," he said.

"Yes, she told me. She told me everything about the two of you: your first smile, the first time you held hands, the way she felt when she kissed you," said Belen.

"Oh," Papa said.

Belen began to get out of the water and came closer to him.

He could see the outline of her shape in the moonlight.

"I often wondered about the stories she told me. I couldn't believe that such a shy boy could kiss so passionately." She gathered her clothes in silence.

"I wish she hadn't told you all of those things. That's kind of personal," Papa said.

"Don't worry. Your secret is safe with me. We're family." She handed him some of the wet clothes to carry back to the camp.

"The water must have been cold," he said.

Belen took one of his hands and blew her warm breath onto it.

He quickly moved his hand away. "What are you doing? Your children are waiting for you." Papa hurried back to the campsite.

"Yes, we mustn't keep everyone waiting. They'll wonder what became of us," she said, giggling.

A few minutes later, they bumped into Daniel.

"There you are! Did you take a bath?" Daniel seemed pleased to smell the soft scent of soap in her wet hair. She had a towel wrapped around her shoulders to hide the wet clothes on her body.

"Yes, my love. Your wife is fresh and clean!" she said, kissing him on the lips.

"I'll leave you two alone," Papa said.

"Where have you been?" Mama asked as Papa came near us.

"We found your sister. She was doing laundry in the dark," he said.

"Not the brightest girl in the bunch, is she?" Mama said, laughing.

"You said it—I didn't," Papa said.

"Sleep by me tonight. The baby has been sleeping well," Mama said.

"I like sleeping by you. Hello, my name is Baldomero," Papa said.

"Funny—come here before she wakes up," Mama said.

Papa crawled next to us, wrapped his arms around Mama, and kissed her gently on the shoulder.

It was a lovely night, warm and calm, and a few gusts of wind made the pecan trees sway from side to side. I could hear the river, which made it easy to fall asleep next to Mama and Papa.

Papa got up early, started the fire, and made breakfast.

I could smell something delicious frying in the iron skillet.

"Baldo?" said Belen.

"Is Daniel awake yet?" he asked.

"Yes, he's been awake for a while. I told him how wonderful the water was last night, and he decided to try it out for himself. You should join him," she said.

"No, I think I'll just start breakfast. We have a long day of hunting ahead of us. I was hoping we could get started right away."

"He'll be back soon. Oh, dear, I feel terrible. I'm so sorry, Baldo," said Belen.

"It's not that big of a deal. We can go tomorrow, I guess. I was hoping to start traveling again soon," Papa said.

"Here, let me do the eggs, and you can flip the bacon." Belen touched Papa's hand and tool the spatula from him.

"I can handle this," he said.

Belen looked at him and kept her hand on his, waiting for him to look at her. She moved her fingers over his hands, keeping her eyes on his face. She waited for a reaction, but he refused to look at her.

He pulled his hand away.

For a long moment, the two remained in silence— and then Belen kissed Papa.

"I always wondered what that would feel like," she said.

Chapter 3

Papa pushed Belen away. "What are you doing?"

"Why are you stopping?" asked Belen.

"Your husband will be here any minute," Papa said.

"I saw how you looked at me the other night when I was in the water." She looked into his eyes for a response.

"I was helping your husband look for you," Papa said.

"You know there was a moment between us," she said.

"I can't believe we are having this conversation! My wife is your sister!" Papa said.

"I know. You'd think I would be able to stop myself, but I can't stop thinking about you." She placed her hand on his cheek.

"Well, you have to! Stay away from me. I can't believe you would do this," Papa said.

"Baldo, don't go," said Belen.

"Don't follow me. I can't believe this is happening," Papa said.

"Baldo, don't walk away. I love you," said Belen.

Papa stopped for a moment and looked at Belen. "If you're going to behave this way, you can't be around me anymore. We'll go ahead of you and Daniel."

"Wait ... please! I'll control myself. You know that my sister needs my help!" said Belen.

"We can manage. It wasn't my idea to have you come along in the first place," Papa said.

"You're right; it was mine," said Belen.

"I thought Daniel wanted you to come. You mean, you could have stayed in town—with Flor and the children?"

"I told him I would leave if he didn't take me with him," she said.

"Don't you love Daniel?" Papa asked.

"Yes, but not like you. Couldn't you see it when I came over every Sunday?" said Belen.

"All this time, I thought you came over to see your sister?"

"And you," said Belen.

"I love my wife," Papa said.

"And you wouldn't have to leave her. You can still be her husband. All I want is to be closer to you," said Belen.

"What is wrong with you?"

"I could take care of you," said Belen coming closer to Papa.

"Stop it," Papa said.

"Stop me," she whispered, kissing him again.

Papa kissed her for a moment, placed his hands on her arms, and pushed her away.

"You do love me." She smiled with tears in her eyes.

"I love my wife," Papa said.

"I'm not jealous," she said.

"I love her—only!"

Belen laughed.

"Why are you laughing?" Papa asked.

"I've never met a man who loved only one woman. My beloved husband looked at other women all the time, after I had children. Who knows what else he did?"

"I've known your husband for years, and I know he would never betray you."

"He betrayed me with his eyes," she said.

"So, is this your revenge? I don't understand. You were just kissing him last night," Papa said.

"I'm tired of pretending. You know I love you," said Belen.

"Belen, you're my sister-in-law," Papa said.

"You kissed me just now, held my hand, and looked at me." Belen came closer and put her hand on his chest.

"Belen, I love my wife. Now, excuse me, but I need to go to her," he said.

"I won't tell her anything," said Belen.

"We've done nothing. There's nothing to tell," Papa said.

"Right … then you shouldn't tell her that you watched me bathing in the moonlight or that you let me kiss you … twice! That might hurt her."

"Leave us alone. I've been listening to you too long. I'm serious. If you hurt my wife, I will make sure you never see us again!"

Papa hurried back to the wagon to be with Mama.

"Where have you been?" Mama asked, waking up.

"I was cleaning up and making breakfast," Papa said.

"Come lie with me before we have to eat," Mama said.

Papa came to Mama and held her closer than ever before.

"You smell like bacon," she said.

Papa held Mama in his arms. "I'm sorry, my love."

"It's okay. I don't mind the smell of bacon. I'll hold you no matter how you smell," Mama said, giggling.

"I'm going to build you a beautiful bed, and a house, and make you the happiest woman alive," Papa said.

"And I can't wait to make you a real meal in our kitchen!" Mama said.

Papa kissed her cheek.

"We've been traveling for so long. Do we have much farther to go?" Mama asked.

"Yes, but think of it as an adventure—a time for us to see things and places we would have never seen had we stayed in Mexico," Papa said.

"Oh, don't say that word! I miss home so much! It's taking longer than we thought, isn't it? People will wonder what happened to us," Mama said.

"We'll see Mexico again, soon enough. Remember, my love, we are each other's home—no matter where we are," Papa said.

He kissed her lips softly and held her tightly.

"I love you so much," Mama said.

In the following days, Papa and Daniel were able to hunt and gather food for our journey.

Papa avoided Belen as much as possible. Wherever she went, he went in the opposite direction.

"Are you mad at Belen?" asked Daniel.

"No," Papa said.

"She mentioned that you act very cold toward her. Did she do something or say something to you?" asked Daniel.

"No. She's just annoying sometimes. No offense," Papa said.

"I guess traveling together can make everyone get on each other's nerves. Don't worry about it. I'll talk to her," Daniel said.

"No—just leave it alone," Papa said.

"Anyway, you know we love you guys. We couldn't have done this trip without you," Daniel said.

"Same here; I can't wait to build our haciendas right next to each other when we get back to Mexico," Papa said, laughing.

"Here's to the future!" Daniel held up a cup of water.

"To the future!" Papa said.

It rained for two days in a row.

Papa had wanted to get started on the trip, but the roads were too muddy. Everyone was ready to get moving again, especially Papa.

Early one morning, Mama heard Belen's children crying outside their wagon.

"What's happening?" Mama asked.

"I'll go look," Papa asked.

"I'd better go with you," Mama said, leaving me on our blanket.

Papa and Mama went to Belen and Daniel's side of the camp to see what was wrong.

"What's the matter?" Papa asked.

My brother and cousins ran to them, and Francisco yelled, "She won't move! Mama won't get up!"

"Belen!" Mama ran to her sister.

Papa tried to hold her back, but Mama had already seen her sister on the floor with a sheet over her face.

"Mama, wake up!" Belen's children wrapped their arms around her limp body.

"Belen!" Mama tried to wake her up, but there was no response.

Papa looked in horror, unable to move.

Mama cried, "Baldo, do something! Isn't there a doctor at the other camp? Where is Daniel?"

"I'll go for the doctor!" Papa ran as fast as he could. He looked around for Daniel, but Daniel was nowhere to be found.

Papa reached the wagon campsite of the doctor and yelled, "Doctor!"

"What is it?" The doctor was cleaning up after breakfast.

"Come quickly! My sister-in-law is not well," Papa said.

"What is it? What do you mean?" asked the doctor.

"I don't know. She's not moving," he said.

"Let's go!" the doctor said.

The two men ran in silence.

"This way, Doctor. There—behind those sheets!"

Mama was still holding her sister close to her chest and rocking her like a child.

The children were crying and screaming for their mother.

"Doctor, please! She's not breathing!" cried Mama.

"Let me see." The doctor gently removed Mama from her sister's side.

"Belen," Mama said, not wanting to let go.

The doctor said, "Baldo, take the children out of here!"

"Where's Daniel?" Papa asked.

"I don't know," Mama said.

"Who is Daniel?" asked the doctor.

"Her husband ... I thought he was with the children earlier," Mama said.

Papa brought the children to the wagon and looked everywhere for Daniel. He took Mama into his arms and tried to help her breathe. She wouldn't speak or leave her sister's side. She held onto her husband, weeping for the death of her lifelong playmate.

The doctor placed a sheet over the young woman again.

Everyone was silent, waiting for the doctor's prognosis.

The doctor looked at Papa with a sorrowful glance.

"Doctor, tell us something," Papa said.

The doctor said, "I'm sorry, my boy."

"She's dead?" Papa asked.

"She can't be dead!" Mama said.

"Where is her husband?" asked the doctor.

"I'm not sure," Papa said.

Daniel was nowhere to be found.

"My sister." Mama was combing her sister's hair back as tears dropped from her eyes.

The doctor took Papa aside so that Mama couldn't hear what he had to say. "She was strangled," he said.

Mama screamed in terror and turned to run away, but she got caught in the sheets that separated the two camps and fell to the ground. As she tried to pick herself up, she noticed something hanging from a tree. "Baldo!"

The doctor and Papa ran over to her, but she was unable to move from where she had fallen. They all looked up at the body hanging from the tree.

The doctor and Papa cut the rope that held Daniel and then sat on the floor to take a breath. Papa was crying for the death of his best friend.

"Baldo?" the doctor said.

"Yes, Doctor?"

"Take your wife to her wagon. This is too much for her to endure. I'm afraid she may go further into shock."

"Of course." Papa tried to remain calm as he led Mama to the wagon and gave her some water.

She wept, still in shock, and was unable to speak.

Papa put me in her arms, and she rocked me and sang to me.

"Baldo?" asked the doctor.

"Yes, doctor?"

"When you're done taking care of your wife, we'll need to find a place to bury the bodies."

"We will need a priest. My wife won't allow them to be buried without a proper burial. I can't believe I'm talking about this," Papa said.

"We will also need to notify the authorities when we get to the nearest town," the doctor said.

"I can't believe this is happening," Papa said.

"Baldo, someone murdered these two souls—and the police need to find out who it was," the doctor said.

Papa remained silent.

"Do you think Daniel could have done this?"

"Done what?" Papa asked.

"Could he have killed his wife and then himself?"

"He loved her," Papa said.

"That's all right. You're probably a little bit in shock as well. Rest a while—and then we'll figure out what to do. Go to your wife."

Papa walked over to Mama and wrapped his arms around her. "Florecita, please, my love, don't cry, the baby needs you."

"My sister is dead. How can my sister be dead?" Mama wept into his chest.

"I don't know, let me hold you. I'm here for you." Papa kissed his wife and wiped away her tears. "We will get through this. I'm here. Hold onto me."

"The children," Mama said. "Where are they?"

"In the other wagon," Papa said.

They ran to the wagon and found the four toddlers crying.

Mama and Papa crawled into the wagon and brought everyone together.

"Shh, there now, everything is going to be fine," Papa said.

"Come here, little ones. Everything is going to be fine," Mama said as she held back her tears.

Everyone gathered around the tiny woman, feeling the warmth and love of her embrace. It became clear to her that, from that day on, she was no longer their aunt; she was their mother.

Chapter 4

Marfa was a small town in West Texas and had been established for a few years. There weren't many Mexicans around those parts, which made us a little bit uncomfortable, but it was the closest place for Papa to buy supplies and find a place for us to rest after everything we had been through.

Dr. Thomas helped us with the funerals and brought us to Marfa to stay at his house for a few days. He was a kind man who lived with his wife and had no children of his own.

Mama now had five children to watch over. She was overwhelmed and unable to keep up with so many mouths to feed. She was still breastfeeding.

Jose was four years old and helped as much as he could. Since Daniel was no longer with them, he tried to be one of the men of the family.

To keep stories from circulating, the funeral was quick. Papa wrote to the families in Mexico about the tragedies and let them know that we would be returning soon. California would have to wait.

"Sometimes I imagine that my sister ran away with Daniel because they were tired of the whole wagon trail, and just needed some time for themselves," Mama said.

"I know ... it's hard to believe," Papa said.

"I'm getting tired of trying to explain to the children what happened to their mother and father," Mama said.

"This has been a shock to all of us," Papa said.

"How could this have happened?" Mama asked.

"At least we have a place to stay. Dr. Thomas's house is very nice. We actually have beds to sleep in. Once the police are done with the investigation, we can head back home. There'll be other chances to go to California, Flor. You'll see. The mountains will always have gold for us."

"All our hopes and dreams have to be put on hold again—and now we have more mouths to feed," Mama said.

"As long as you are safe, and we have each other, nothing else matters," Papa said.

One day, while the children played and Mama was cleaning up our room, there was a knock at the door.

"Let me go see who it is." Dr. Thomas opened the door.

A tall man with a gun around his waist and a badge on his chest said, "Are you Baldomero?"

"Yes?" Papa asked.

"Hello. I'm Officer Bailey. Pardon the intrusion, but we just have a few questions about what happened to your in-laws a few days ago. Dr. Thomas told us what happened, but we just wanted to make sure about the details."

"Yes," Papa said.

"So, Baldomero, may I call you by your first name?"

"Baldo is fine," Papa said.

"Did you know if there was anyone who wanted to do harm to your sister-in-law and her husband?"

"No," Papa said.

"Was there anyone who Daniel might have been having problems with … maybe another person at the campsite or wagon trail?"

"No," Papa said.

"Were there any problems between Daniel and his wife?"

Papa hesitated and then said, "No."

"Are you sure?"

"Yes," Papa said.

The officer wrote something down in his book. "Do you think Daniel might have physically harmed his wife?"

Mama had been listening from our room. "Daniel loved his wife!" she said in Spanish. She couldn't speak English, but she could understand some of what was being said.

"Florecita, you should stay in the bedroom," Papa said.

"What are they trying to say?" she asked in Spanish. "Daniel loved his wife."

"What did she say?" asked the officer.

"Sorry. She doesn't speak English. She said, 'Daniel loved his wife.'"

Mama said, "Belen loved her husband just as she had from the day she met him by the Ojo de Dios. They were together since the day they met, and they loved each other more than anyone she'd ever known."

"Excuse me … my wife is very upset," Papa said.

The officer said, "Sorry to upset your wife. Could we talk outside?"

"Yes," Papa said.

"Come, Baldo. This is just the routine," Dr. Thomas said.

Mama and the rest of us stayed inside.

After an hour, Papa came back inside.

"What happened?" Mama asked.

"Just questions," he answered.

"Questions? About what?"

"That day …"

"Baldo, I have to tell you something," Mama said.

Papa looked at her and said, "What?"

"First, let me make sure everyone is asleep. I kept your food warm. Eat something and I'll meet you in bed."

Papa stared at the fireplace.

When Mama got in bed, she held him with all her might.

"What is it?" Papa asked.

"I heard them fighting," Mama said.

"Who?" Papa asked.

"Daniel and Belen," she said.

"What were they fighting about?"

Mama paused. "Daniel kept saying that he heard you and Belen talking in the woods by yourselves … and something about what she had written in her journal."

"Journal?"

"She was prettier than me, wasn't she, Baldo?" Mama asked.

Papa held Mama. "That's ridiculous. You are lovely. You mean everything to me."

"Daniel said he saw you looking at her shape in the water," Mama said.

"Florecita! You're the only woman I have ever loved. Please believe me when I say this!"

"Maybe you were tired of me always saying no to you because I was so exhausted from taking care of the children," Mama said.

"No," Papa said.

"Perhaps my sister could give you more attention than I could," Mama said.

"No! I mean, we spoke a couple times, but I should have never let her speak to me. I didn't know how to stop her without insulting her."

"Stop her from doing what?"

Papa stayed silent.

"Do you still love me?" Mama asked.

"Yes, I only love you. Do you know how much I have hated myself for having betrayed you—even if it was just for a moment? I can't stand myself! But I couldn't lose you, Florecita, that's why I never told you. I didn't want to hurt you."

"How did you betray me?" Mama asked.

"I stopped it before anything could happen. I couldn't look at her as anything but your sister. Look at me. I love you! Nothing happened," Papa said.

"Nothing?" Mama asked.

Papa looked at Mama, and tears began pouring out of his eyes. "Please forgive me." He placed his head by her heart.

Mama stood up, looked down at her husband, and said, "I know it hurts. Trust me when I say that pain is good. It teaches us to keep from repeating past mistakes. Shh … Baldo, don't cry my love." Mama placed her hands on his cheeks. "I already forgave you."

"If you have forgiven me, it is because you know that I truly love you," Papa said.

"I do," Mama said.

Chapter 5

For the next few weeks, we stayed in Marfa, and the police continued the investigation.

Papa told Mama it was best to keep quiet and let them come to their own conclusions with whatever evidence they had.

Mama continued learning how to be a mother of five.

Papa found a job working in the fields for the time being. He was exhausted at the end of the day, and his young hands were becoming scratched and bruised.

"Mama, when is Papa coming home?" Jose said, my older brother.

"He'll be home tonight," answered Mama.

"Why can't I go with him? I could help him," Jose said.

"He'll be fine, my love. When he comes home, we'll give him big hugs—and I will pour warm water on his hands," Mama said.

"And when are we going to Colorado or California or wherever we were supposed to be?" Jose said.

"Soon—that's why Papa is working. We will have plenty of money to buy food and have everything we need for our trip."

"So, we're still going?" Jose said.

"We are not staying here. The good doctor has been so good to us, but we need to go home first. We'll go to California some other time," Mama said.

"Mama, why did Belen and Daniel die?" Jose said.

Mama looked into his large brown eyes, unable to breathe for a moment. "Your aunt died because she could not breathe well."

"She was breathing fine the day before," Jose said.

"She choked suddenly, and we were not able to save her," Mama said.

"How did Uncle Daniel die?"

"Daniel was so sad that his beloved wife died that he decided to go with her," Mama said.

"Go with her where? Into the ground?"

"No, to heaven," Mama said.

"Why did they leave their children behind?"

"I don't know. Come here." She held Jose in her arms. "Sometimes it's better to leave things in the past and think more about the future." She kissed his chubby cheeks and laid him down next to his cousins. She covered everyone with an extra blanket and lay down by me on the blanketed floor.

An hour or so later, Mama carefully got up to greet Papa at the door with kisses and hugs. She led him to the fire to put new bandages on his old scratches and cleaned the cuts he'd received that day. She took off his shoes and washed his feet and legs.

Papa whispered to her all the things that he did that day and took out a few coins.

She placed the coins in a tin under the bed.

He looked at her with hope and thankfulness for everything she had done for him—even after he'd hurt her so much. "We made much progress today."

"Really?" Mama said with a smile.

"Yes. The foreman seems to like that I'm younger and stronger than some of the others."

"Is that why you're so torn up? Because you're trying to show off?" Mama giggled.

"It's not funny! This is hard work!" Papa said.

Mama said, "I'm just playing with you. I know it's hard, but you have to be more careful! When we begin traveling again, you'll need to have strong hands for the reins—unless you want me to handle the horses while you breastfeed!"

"Right," Papa said.

"All right then, I need you to stop getting yourself all scratched up!" Mama said.

"How much do you need me?" Papa asked.

"Like my lungs need air," she said, smiling.

He smiled back and kissed his wife.

"Let's go to sleep," Mama said.

Papa said, "Soon, we'll be on our way home, and then I will go to California with some friends. It's safer that way. Just give me a few more days to make money for our trip."

Mama said, "I was so ready to smell the ocean and feel the sand under my feet. I still dream of us there, holding hands and running in the water."

"Yes, Florecita—very soon, those won't be dreams anymore. With everything we've been through, God has to help us out."

"He's helped us get this far." Mama kissed Papa, and he cuddled her gently in his arms.

The next morning, Papa got up and dressed for work.

Mama made him his usual breakfast before feeding everyone else. She gave him a hearty lunch, kissed him full on the lips, and held him one more time. "Take care of yourself. Come back to me with fewer cuts on your hands!"

After washing our faces and brushing the teeth of those who had teeth, Mama prepared us for a walk around the block. It was our daily exercise and a moment of fresh air for Mama.

When we came back to the house, a police officer was looking through Belen's things.

"What are you doing here?" she asked.

"Hello," said the officer. "I'm sorry to intrude, but we had someone come into town with a very interesting story the other day, which made me a little curious. Some camper saw your sister and her husband arguing about something the night of the murder."

She couldn't understand a thing he was saying. With her best English, Mama said, "Please come later."

He wouldn't leave. He looked everywhere—even going through our clothes and things that belonged to Belen.

Mama just kept repeating, "Please ... come later."

"Is this her journal?" asked the officer.

When Mama saw her sister's journal in his hand, she stopped breathing.

"Baldo—isn't that your husband's name?"

Mama couldn't understand anything, but hearing her husband's name as the officer read from Belen's diary helped her understand that Belen had written about Papa.

"Is it possible that your husband loved Belen and killed Daniel for killing Belen? Maybe Daniel read her diary. I'll need someone to translate this."

"Please ... come later," Mama said.

Finally, the officer agreed to come back later, taking the journal with him.

Mama waited until the officer was out of view and walked quickly to the doctor's main house. "Doctor!" Mama was crying as she tried to speak.

"Florecita! Are you all right? What did the officer say to you?" the doctor said in his best Spanish.

"I have to go to Baldo! I have to tell him something! Please, can your wife stay with my children?"

"Are you all right? Are you sure you wouldn't prefer that I go?"

"No, there is something I must tell him," she said.

When the doctor saw that Mama was determined to do this on her own, he didn't refuse her request and quickly went to his wife.

Mama came back to our room and gathered a few of Papa's things. She put a loaf of bread and some clothes and money in a bag.

The fields weren't far from where we stayed, and Mama took one of the horses and went as quickly as she could to find Papa. She found him working close to a fence. "Baldo!"

He quickly ran to her. "What is it?"

"You have to go! The police came today and took Belen's journal. It had your name in it."

"Why did he take it? So what if my name was in it? I did nothing! Remember I was with you all night!"

"But what if they think you did it? Who knows what she wrote? Just go where they can't find you. And when you're far away enough, we will come to you. You will send for us, and we will come in a few days. I've packed your things for you."

"I won't leave you—and leaving will only make me look guilty of something!"

"We can't stay here!" she said.

"I won't leave you!"

"It's just for a little while. You need to get out of here! I won't let them accuse you of something you didn't do."

"Come with me!" Papa kissed her hands.

"I have a horse waiting for you over there. You will send for us! I need time to get the children ready. Go!" She kissed him again quickly and held him closely one last time before she pulled herself away.

"I love you," he yelled.

"I love you!" she cried as she ran back to her children.

After several yards, she stopped to look back. As Baldo moved farther away, she fell to the floor. "You will send for us," she whispered.

Chapter 6

We were lucky to be able to live with the doctor until we heard from Papa. After a few weeks went by, Mama stopped looking out the window every minute. "Something must have happened," she said.

At first, we thought she'd never leave the front room. She would clean one room, and then she would go to the living room to look at the window. She waited for a letter from the postman or a messenger. When nothing came, she would go clean another room and come back a few minutes later to look out the window.

"Can you see Papa?" Jose said.

"Papa is going to send for us. I need to be on the lookout for someone who might have a message for us," she whispered.

"Where is he?" he asked.

Mama said, "Somewhere safe. We are going to go to him when he lets us know where he is. Don't worry, my dear. We will be with your papa soon. But listen to me, we must keep this between us, okay?"

Jose nodded.

The doctor came into the room and said, "Florecita, the meal you made last night was incredible!"

"Gracias," Mama said.

"My wife wants you to teach her how to cook," the doctor said.

"I would be glad to teach her. I only know a few dishes, but they are easy to learn," she said.

"Oh, I don't know," Mrs. Mary said. The doctor's wife also knew Spanish and French. "Well, I guess I could try. And maybe I can teach you how to make French food."

"That would be nice. Thank you," Mama said.

Mama and Mrs. Mary worked together in the kitchen at least one night per week. They learned new things from each other, and Mama kept her eyes on the window at the front of the house.

One night, while the two women were knitting mittens for the children, Mama looked out as she always did.

"Your husband has been gone for some time," Mrs. Mary said.

"He had some business to take care of," Mama said.

"My husband told me a little of your story. I'm sorry if he should have kept it to himself, but I was so worried about you."

"That's all right. I guess I'm looking to see if my husband is looking at us through the trees," she said.

"He probably needs time to get things settled for you to meet him," Mrs. Mary said.

"But it's been so long," Mama said.

"Well, you know, traveling these days is difficult. He'll need to find a job to feed all of these mouths. He probably knows you're better off here until he can send for you."

"I suppose you're right. It's just that this is the first time we've ever been apart," Mama said as tears began to form in her eyes.

"Oh, dear, let's talk about something else. How did you meet?"

"Well, we grew up in a village called Tarandacuao, Mexico. I used to swim in this place where the water was deep. I would jump off the cliff to show off for him. While I was trying to convince my sister to try it, we both saw him jump off and dive in like an eagle. He was amazing. When he didn't come up for a few seconds, I jumped in to see if he was all right—and of course he was."

Mama did everything she could to keep busy so that the days wouldn't seem as long.

We'd wake up early in the morning, eat breakfast, and then clean the house. The two eldest children, Jose and Elida, who were about the same age, helped Mama with breakfast.

Mama made tortillas from scratch. They were always perfectly round and never had burned spots. They were the fluffiest tortillas around.

"Florecita, where did you get the recipe for these tortillas?" asked the doctor. He would eat three or four at every meal.

"My mother—she is an excellent cook," Mama said.

"You must teach my wife how to make these," Dr. Thomas said.

Mrs. Mary said, "Oh, yes! The only problem with that is that my husband has gained a few pounds—and I'm trying to keep my waistline from getting any bigger!"

"My darling, you could be any size, and I would love every inch of you." Dr. Thomas kissed his wife on the cheek and wrapped his arms around her waist.

"You are too kind, monsieur," she said as he walked out the door. "I apologize, Florecita. We are so insensitive. I know how you miss your husband. I try to think of what it would be like to be without my husband, and it makes me shiver."

"Please don't apologize. You must enjoy every minute you have with him. I just wish I had spent more time with mine. I feel like I'll never see him again."

Mrs. Mary said, "You will be together in no time! He has a wife and five children who are his life. How can you think he would never come back to you?"

"He's never been gone this long. It hurts when I reach for him at night—and he's not there."

"He'll be back, Florecita," Mrs. Mary said.

"That police officer won't stop asking about him. We should have gone with him, but there was no time!"

"Florecita, stop! You can't worry about such things! My goodness! Think positively! He's probably on his way to Colorado or California, trying to find a job so that he can send for you and the children. Won't that be wonderful?" Mrs. Mary dried Mama's tears.

"That would be wonderful. I just wish I knew for sure," Mama said.

"Look, when he sends for you, we will all pretend to take a trip. We will take you to wherever he is. If anyone asks, we'll just say we need our best cook to come with us. That will be you and your children of course!"

"You would do that for us?" Mama asked.

Mrs. Mary laughed and said, "Don't be silly! I would love to get out of Marfa!"

"Why?" Mama asked.

"Have you looked around? There's nothing here but ranchers and oil, and that's about it. Oh, Florecita, if you could only see where I grew up, you would know why I want to leave here."

"What is it like in France?" Mama asked.

"I lived in Giverny, which is nothing like this place. It is very green, and there are trees everywhere. People move much slower, and they read and paint. Music is everywhere. French food and wine are what I think they serve in heaven."

"That sounds like Tarandacuao," Mama said.

"Really?"

"Yes. Except they make tequila instead of wine. I never drank it much," Mama said.

"Why did we ever leave?"

"To be with our husbands?"

"I suppose. Would you like some wine from France? My parents send me some from time to time."

"That would be nice. Thank you," Mama said.

"We'll serve it at dinner tonight. What should we make? You need to teach me how to make tortillas and ... the stuffed peppers you made the other night!"

"Chiles rellenos?"

"Yes!"

"Okay. We'll need to go to the market," Mama said.

"Then let's go! I'll get the girls ready, and you get the boys," Mrs. Mary said.

"Very well," Mama said.

At the market, they smelled green peppers until they found the right amount of spiciness and sweetness. For the little ones, they bought plenty of vegetables and beef to make stew that Mama called *carne guisada*.

Mama remembered how chiles rellenos was one of the things she used to attract her husband. Not that he needed an excuse—for his love was already increasing by the day—but they were what brought him to his knees.

"What are you making?" Mama remembered Papa asking on the day he came to dine at their house years ago.

"You'll see," she said with a smile.

"Can I watch?" Papa should have been playing horseshoes outside with the other men.

"You can help me," Mama said.

"What do I do?" he asked as he washed his hands.

"Take those chiles and wash them well. Then toast them on the comal until the skin burns just a little," Mama said.

"But what if they burn?"

"A little burn never hurt," Mama said.

He did as she instructed and handed her the peppers. She showed him how to use his fingers to peel away the charred skin, and then she cut one of the peppers and removed the seeds and stem. She breathed its spicy aroma as she looked at Papa. After she stuffed ground beef, cheese, and onions into the peppers, she sewed it closed and told Papa to beat some egg whites. "Make sure that you beat them until you can make a mountain at the top."

"Is this good?" he asked, showing her his handiwork.

"Good," she said as she looked into his brown eyes. She took the bowl from him and dipped each pepper into the flour and then into the fluffy egg whites. She let them sizzle in bubbling oil until they were golden brown.

Papa moved toward her and kissed her lips while her hands were occupied.

Her flirting had worked, but now she was a lovely shade of pink.

During the meal, Mama stared at her food, unable to speak, and Papa stared at her from across the table.

"Florecita?" Mrs. Mary said.

"Yes? Oh, I'm sorry. I was thinking about something," Mama said.

"You're turning red," Mrs. Mary said with a smile.

Mama laughed, knowing that Mrs. Mary understood where her thoughts might have been. "It must be the chiles," Mama said.

"Mmm-hmm," Mrs. Mary said, laughing.

Mama volunteered to cook every day to spend time reliving her days with Papa. It was her way of visiting with him.

One weekend, she decided to visit her sister's and brother-in-law's graves after church. It had been some time since she had been able to do so. "Hello, sister," Mama said. "I just wanted to bring you the good news about your children. They are doing very well and beginning to talk more every day. Francisco smiles all the time. He and Rosa play well together. Jose and the girls are getting ready to take lessons from Mrs. Mary. She is very educated and will surely teach them well. Hello, Daniel. You should be proud. They are very well behaved and play together well. As for your friend and my husband, I have not heard anything in a little less than a year. He let me know that he did not love your wife. He was weak, but he did not love her. He loves me. And I know that she loved you. You were all she talked about when we were growing up. I spoke to the priest here, and he said if I pray for you, you could be spared from going to hell. So here it goes.

"Dear God, forgive my brother-in-law, Daniel, for taking his own life and the life of my sister. He spent his life serving you. I'm sorry he went mad in his final hours, but he was a good man. Forgive also Belen for trying to take away my husband. Lord, forgive me for being bitter. Forgive me for being ungrateful. Thank you for the children and how healthy and good they are. Thank you for giving us such a nice place to live and people to share a home with. Bless the doctor and his wife and give them everything they need. Lord, thank you for my husband. Watch over him so that we may be together again. God, bring him back to me."

She wept until she fell asleep by the graves of her dead relatives. She didn't feel much more alive than those who were six feet below her.

Chapter 7

Mama began working at a hotel on the weekends, cooking meals for guests.

We stayed with Mrs. Mary, and she tutored the older children and taught them how to read.

While Mama was sweeping outside, a man walked up to the hotel. He seemed like he'd been riding for some time. He was Hispanic, dusty, and sunburned. She wondered where he could be coming from, and she pretended to be cleaning the hotel lobby to find out.

The clerk said, "Hello."

"Yes. May I have a room for the night?" the gentleman said.

"Yes, sir. That will be five dollars." The clerk stared at the man's dirty boots.

"Thank you—and here is a little for you." The gentleman gave a generous tip to the clerk.

"This way please. You will be in room 7," the clerk said.

That evening, Mama prepared a hearty meal of enchiladas, tortillas de *maiz*, carne guisada, and arroz con *cebolla* y maiz. She was hoping the smell of the peppers and rich sauces would bring the man out so that she might serve him and perhaps see if she knew anything about Papa. That was one reason she began working at the hotel. It gave her a place to inquire about her husband.

"Buenas noches," said the gentleman as he walked into the dining room.

"Buenas noches." Mama brought him a plate of her scrumptious food.

"Are you from here?" asked the man in her native language.

"No, we are from Tarandacuao," she said, looking at her apron. She hated making eye contact with strangers. Men treated women as if they belonged to them, and Hispanic men, in particular, always thought a pretty girl was their prize.

"Tarandacuao?"

"Yes," she said. Not many people traveled from Tarandacuao, and if this man had ever spoken to Papa, he might have told him about it.

"I used to go to Ojo de Dios in 'Taranda.' I have fond memories of swimming there with my cousin," said the man.

She smiled.

"You have a beautiful smile. I was wondering if I would get to see it," he said. "Pedro Chavez is my name." He leaned over and whispered, "I am your husband's cousin, Florecita."

Mama was unable to speak.

"You must be wondering how I found you," he said.

"Do you know anything about Baldo?" she asked.

"I know that he is alive and sends you his love," he said.

"Where is he?" She waited to for an answer so she could get on a horse and go to him as quickly as possible.

"He is in a little town named Celina, which is not far from here. He was in jail for some time for stealing food from a store. Since our family had not heard from any of you in some time, they sent me to look for you. It took me some time because I went on the trail you were supposed to take. I couldn't understand why you had been gone so long without any word. So, I began inquiring with the law to see if there had been any trouble, but no one had heard anything until I reached the hills. That's where I heard about what happened.

"I was going to another town, but someone said they had the best *enchiladas* at this hotel. You know how many hotels in West Texas have Mexican food? Not many. If they have it, it's not good. Not at all." He smiled.

"Please tell me about my husband!"

Pedro said, "I recently came back from the mines in Zacatecas and had quite a bit of luck there with the silver. So, when I heard about my cousin, I knew it would be a good idea to help him out. Don't worry. He's fine."

Mama thanked God in her heart.

"Your family has been worried about all of you," he said.

Mama began to walk away. "Thank you for the information. Please, excuse me."

"Let me know if you need any help," Pedro said.

Mama quickly gathered her things, told the manager that she needed to go home, and ran to the doctor's house, which was only a few blocks away. She was crying hysterically. She gathered me in her arms, kissed me tenderly on my forehead, and touched my face.

The other children gathered around us.

Mrs. Mary said, "Flor, why are you in such a state? What happened?"

"There was this man at the hotel. He says he's my husband's cousin and that he's seen Baldo, but I don't know if I can trust him." Mama's hugs were becoming uncomfortable.

Mrs. Mary said, "All right, everyone, leave your mama for a minute. She must have had a long, hard day of cooking and needs some rest." She gathered all the children to take them to the parlor. "Would you like me to take Rosa so that you can rest?"

"No," Mama said, holding on to me.

"All right," Mrs. Mary said, leaving us alone. "Rosa?"

"Mama." It was one of the few words I knew.

"You know that I love you," she said.

"Mama." I held her face in my little hands.

"You are one of my greatest joys." She held me closer.

I didn't know what to say. I just let her hold me until she stopped crying. She probably thought she was frightening me just a little, but I didn't mind. I wasn't good at doing much yet, but hugging was my specialty.

The next day, Mama took me and the other children to visit Mrs. Mary's mother in a town called Fredericksburg. She said there were many German settlers, and they were very friendly because they were also new to this land.

"We'll be here for a few weeks," Mrs. Mary said.

"Thank you so much. I'll probably lose my job at the hotel," Mama said.

"I doubt it. Besides, you've been there almost a year, and you've never taken a vacation. My husband plays poker with the owner, and he said being without your enchiladas would be torture."

"I don't know how to thank you. That man at the hotel was creepy. I just don't know who to trust anymore. What if he was working for the police and trying to get information from me?" Mama held my hand snuggly.

"Fredericksburg is a lovely place to visit. It will get all of that off your mind. You'll love the green hills, and the Germans enjoy lovely festivals. Don't worry. If your husband sends a message, my husband will bring it to us immediately."

Mrs. Mary's mother was called Mrs. Charlotte. "So how did you meet this girl?"

Mrs. Mary said, "She came to us quite tragically, I'm afraid. You see, there was a death in the family, or rather two." She whispered to her mother while Mama gave the children a bath. Mrs. Mary played with me while she spoke to her mother.

"Oh, dear," said Mrs. Charlotte.

"*Oui*, Mama. This girl has been through so much. I don't know how she manages to stay sane. It's as if, every time she turns around, someone is taken away from her."

"So, what happened?" asked Mrs. Charlotte.

"Flor and her husband had been traveling with Flor's sister and her family. Along the way, her husband and her sister began a flirtation—and the husband got wind of it."

"Good heavens, the sister and the husband?"

"Yes. But Flor still believes her husband was innocent and that her sister seduced him."

"I see," Mrs. Charlotte said.

"That's how she feels, and we won't say anything about it," Mrs. Mary said.

"So, did the husband and sister run away together? I notice neither of them is here."

"The sister is dead, and Flor's husband is nowhere to be found," Mrs. Mary said.

"Oh my."

"She was killed by her own husband after he found out about the two of them. Then he hung himself!"

"My goodness. What a horror!"

Mrs. Mary said, "I know. She works at a nearby hotel while I teach the children. We all needed a break."

"And the husband is nowhere to be found? Why did he leave?"

"The police took the dead woman's journal, and it mentioned Flor's husband. Flor had no idea what they were thinking and thought it was best if he just left. I don't blame her. The police have never been fair to anyone different."

"Why didn't you tell me this before?"

"I suppose it was too much to tell in a letter," Mrs. Mary said.

"You and your husband are good people," said Mrs. Charlotte.

"My husband had been doing some work out by the hills where people camped. He thought he would be treating patients with cuts. He never thought he would be burying bodies."

"And now?"

"Now we just wait and see if her husband will return. Mama, it's been over a year now and not a word," said Mary.

"For all you know he could be ..."

"Don't even breathe those words, Mama. He's alive somewhere. He will come back to her," said Mary.

"He'd better come back to that sweet girl."

A few days later, after swimming in the river almost every day, eating sausage almost every night, and playing with the goats on Mrs. Charlotte's farm, Mrs. Mary decided it was time for all of us to get back to Marfa.

"Thank you so much for your wonderful cooking, Flor," said Mrs. Charlotte.

"You are welcome, Mrs. Charlotte. Your daughter is also cooking well," Mama said.

"Yes, I noticed she was also handy in the kitchen." Mrs. Charlotte gave her daughter a hug and a kiss.

"Au revoir, Mama," Mrs. Mary said.

"Au revoir, everyone. Come back and feed my goats anytime!"

Mrs. Mary's driver let us sit up front with him, but with five children, we all had to take turns. Mama snuggled me most of the way, and Jose sat close by.

My sisters were good to us as well. It was a joy to be surrounded by people around my size and feeling safe with my family.

When we arrived in Marfa, there was a letter waiting for Mama. She took it into her hands and looked at it as if it would speak to her. Holding it to her heart, she waited until she was alone to read it.

Mrs. Mary waited patiently until the door finally opened. "What did it say?"

"He's alive!" Mama said as tears of relief streamed down her face.

"What?" Mrs. Mary said.

"Yes. That man who came here—the one I thought was scary—wrote the letter. He really is my husband's cousin and was sent to look for us. He was telling the truth! He helped get Baldo out of jail by bribing a guard, but Baldo had to promise not to come back for a year. Baldo sent him to warn me that he would be coming back to me soon."

"But won't it be dangerous for him to come back here? It's been a year, but he might still be a wanted man."

"I know. We will have to leave, Mrs. Mary," Mama said. Marfa was the only place we had called home since we left Mexico.

"Where will you go? You have to let us help you. I will speak to my husband and see if we have relatives somewhere else where you can stay. Perhaps you could work for them."

"I appreciate any help we can get. Oh, Mary, I can't wait to see him! You don't know what it's like waking up with five children by your side—and no husband! I know it sounds selfish, and I love my children, but I can't live another day without my husband."

"I know. Come to think of it, we have relatives in Celina. They own a hotel. They may be able to help us."

"You mean help me and my family. You mustn't involve yourselves, Mrs. Mary. I would die if anything happened to you or the doctor."

Mary held Mama's hand and said, "We're your family, Rosa. We may not be related, but we have shared a home and have saved each other from sheer boredom! How will I live without seeing those five little faces sitting around my table?"

Mama thought she had been a burden to that wonderful couple, but she now realized how much she and the children had filled their lives. She put her arms around Mary. "Well, then we will definitely see each other again when you come to visit in Celina. Be prepared for an abundance of hugs and kisses."

"They'll forget me," Mrs. Mary said. "They are so little."

"I won't let them," Mama said as she smiled at the woman who had become her sister.

Chapter 8

Celina, Texas, was another dusty town—with even fewer trees than Marfa. We had lived there now for more than a decade. The dreams of reaching California had been blown away by the Texas wind.

There was a Catholic church and a Baptist church. There was a school for Americans—but none for anyone else—and a large crater in the middle of the town for digging dirt and cement. Nearby, there was a white gazebo with a little park around it. Not much to see.

On the other side of the hole were the houses of a few Mexican people who came to this dusty town. Perhaps they too had heard of opportunity in the United States of America. Maybe they had also been on their way to California and somehow gotten sidetracked.

What was so bad about Mexico and its beautiful mountains, glorious beaches, and tropical and abundant lands? It had some of the greenest places on the Earth. How I wished we could see our homeland.

As we were drinking soda on our front porch, Elida said, "I don't understand it."

"You don't understand what?" I asked.

"Maybe we are luckier to live in a land where revolution and civil war aren't a threat like they are in

Mexico. But here, it's a different kind of war. It's a war of color. Natives whose skin was darker than mine—people who said the land belonged to God—were here before everyone else."

"Sometimes I call myself Rose instead of Rosa," I admitted.

Elida said, "Be proud of who you are, little sister. I know it's hard, but you have to. Otherwise, they win."

"I understand English. It helps if you know English at work. One time I was sent to a ladies' room because she needed her dress ironed. She was so glamorous, and she gave me a good tip. I said, 'Thank you!' in English."

"Try working in the kitchen! Talk about work," Francisco said.

"At least we have jobs," said Elena.

Papa was with us, working our farm and keeping his family together. Mama worked closely by him. I sometimes wondered if this was because of how long he'd been gone that year when we lived in Marfa.

My eldest brother, Francisco, was about to be married to a girl we'd known from the hotel.

Jose and I were the youngest. We spent summers swimming in the water tank in the middle of the night because we weren't allowed to swim in the public pool, but I was happier having the whole tank to ourselves. I became an excellent swimmer and could climb a water tank faster than my brother could.

As we swam, Jose said, "Can you believe how big this wedding is going to be?"

I said, "Francisco is so in love it makes me sick. Margarita needs to get him out of the house!"

"Are you excited to be a flower girl?"

"Not at all," I said.

"Well, at least I'll get a bedroom all to myself."

"We'll see about that," I said.

Jose splashed water in my face.

"I have to see Margarita tomorrow about flowers," I said.

Jose laughed. "I can't wait to hear all about it."

The next day, Margarita said, "Oh! Don't my flowers look perfect, Rosa?"

"Yes, I've never seen roses at a wedding before," I said under my breath.

"You should be happy we chose roses. You know, like your name!"

I could tell she was trying to be my friend, but it wasn't working.

"So, anyway, I'm going to need you to make those wonderful tortillas you and Mama make so well. They are just the best in the world. Can you do that for me, sweet baby sister?"

I cringed at the thought that she would be part of the family very soon. It wasn't that I didn't like her; it was that she was better friends with my older sisters than me I was.

My sisters were older and looked like twins. They met boys at the same time, and they shared dresses because they were both the same size. I was the oddball who never quite fit in.

"Sure, it will be a pleasure to cook for your wedding," I said.

"I'm so glad your sisters are going to be my bridesmaids. They look perfect in the dresses I chose," said Margarita.

I knew it wouldn't be such a bad idea to be stuck in the kitchen. I wasn't in the mood to mingle with all the guests.

"Oh, look! It's Francisco. You'd better get going so I can get started on figuring out how much dough we will need for the tortillas. Do you want flour, corn, or both?"

"Both," she said.

"Of course," I said.

She smiled and tilted her head as if to say thank you with her gesture.

That night, my sisters were getting ready for some event that I was not invited to. I accidentally walked in on them and said, "Where are you two going?"

Even though they had their own houses right next door to each other, they were getting ready in my mother's room.

"Well, we didn't want to tell you, but Margarita invited us to have a little get-together before her wedding tomorrow and, you know, do girl stuff."

They giggled as they put Mother's makeup on their faces.

Mama walked in and said, "What are you doing in here?"

"Mama!" They walked up to her and each gave her a kiss on the cheek. "We were just borrowing some things for tonight. We knew you wouldn't mind."

"Where are you three going?" Mama asked.

"Not three, Mama. Margarita only invited Elida and me," said Elena.

"Why not Rosa?" Mama asked.

"Well, you know, she's … younger," said Elida.

Mama looked at the two girls and said, "That's fine. We're all eating together tomorrow for dinner— so don't be late or your father will come looking for you." Mama put her arm around me as we walked out of her room together.

As they left, Elida whispered, "Mama always preferred her more."

Elena said, "I wonder what it would have been like if we had grown up with our *real* mother."

I stopped moving and looked at Mama. I could barely see in the darkened hallway, but she looked at me with her dark eyes. "What did they mean by *real* mother?"

"They're just being silly," Mama said.

"No, they were being serious," I said.

"Rosa, don't worry about them. We have to plan the food for the wedding."

"Mama, it's okay. If you don't want to tell me why they said that, I understand."

"Come with me, Rosa. I want to show you something," Mama said as we walked out of the house.

Chapter 9

Mama said nothing the whole time we walked to the gazebo.

Celina was on very flat land. There were so many pecan trees on the hill overlooking the hole in the ground. Our house was built higher than the rest of the town, making the crater look especially deep.

Mama took a deep breath and looked down at her soft, weathered hands. "Your father and I came from Tarandacuao, Guanajuato, many years ago, just a few days after you were born." She stopped for a moment to let the wind die down.

I made sure not to interrupt.

"We were on our way to California to find our fortune. There were stories of gold and silver shining in the rivers, between the mountains. I was so excited to see a river shining with gold. I couldn't think of anything else but all the things I would be able to buy for you and for our little family. Your papa was the kindest, sweetest young man you could ever imagine. He was full of hope and dreams. I mean, he is still kind, but certain memories have made him older than he should be."

I wasn't sure what she meant about my father being different from what he used to be. He seemed fine to me, and I loved him very much.

"When we first came to America, your father was sent to jail for a crime he didn't commit."

"Why?"

"He was accused of stealing bread," Mama said.

"That's it? Well, that's not so bad," I said.

"That's not all. He was also suspected in the murder of your aunt."

"You had a sister?" I asked.

"I had a sister named Belen. And, no, your father did not kill her. She was beautiful. She had dark skin, high cheekbones, black eyes, and dark, wavy hair, like your sisters."

"She's their real mother, right?"

"Yes. I took over as their mother after she died. I thought I would tell you someday, but there's never been a good time. I'm sorry for keeping this from you, Rosa."

"Is it because you still think I'm a little girl?"

"In some ways, you'll always be my baby. Even when you're an old lady, you'll be my little girl." Mama kissed my hand.

"What about your parents? You never talk about them either."

She looked away. "They died few years ago."

"I'm sorry, Mama."

"I know your sisters have not always been kind to you. Big sisters can be that way. Even though they have been given the same affection, they resent you because I always loved you more ... since you are truly mine ... you and Jose."

"So, Francisco is also my cousin?" I felt a little sick.

"He is, but he loves you so much. He's always been your protective big brother. I thought they were all too little when this happened, but Elida remembers. She must have been in shock in the beginning, but she remembers. When she was twelve, she became angry with me for not letting her go to the gazebo to see Mauricio. That's when she yelled out that she knew I was not her real mother."

"That sounds like Elida. Anything to see her boyfriend. So, who did kill my aunt?"

"Their father," Mama said.

"Why?"

"There is the kind of love that lives with you forever—and the kind of love that lasts only a moment. Your father and I found the love that lasts forever, and it withstands even those moments that could have torn us apart."

"But what did this have to do with Papa stealing bread?"

"Daniel, your uncle, found Belen's diary. I think she proclaimed her love to your father in that diary. It drove Daniel into a rage, and he killed her—and then himself."

The tree hovering over us moved like a spirit that wanted to say something. The wind whispered in my ear, "I loved him." I knew it was the spirit of Belen.

Mama said, "I told him to leave because I thought the police would think he had something to do with the murder. It just made him seem more suspicious. That's why he was gone for about a year. It was the worst year of my life."

I said, "So, my sisters and brothers are my cousins, and I had an aunt and uncle who died in a terrible murder-suicide?"

"Yes," Mama said.

"That's a lot," I said, looking at the ground.

Mama said, "The reason I brought you here was so that you could meet them. These are only the tombstones; their bodies are far from here."

I read the tombstone: "Beloved husband and wife, Belen and Daniel."

She said, "I knew Daniel would have liked that."

I walked in silence with Mama, pondering everything she had told me.

We came home late that evening, after continuing our walk through the town, talking about the wedding and the future. We left the past in the past.

The wedding would be a grand ceremony in the Catholic church with a home-cooked meal and a reception around the gazebo. Everyone who wanted to come was invited.

I was a little jealous of the whole thing, never having experienced love myself, but my mother told me it wasn't my time yet.

Thirteen-year-old boys are not attractive at all. They smell like sweat and dirt. How could anyone love that? I will marry someone like my father. He is a hardworking, honorable man who loves his family and treats me like his favorite. I adore him. No matter what happened in the past, I know he loved my mother.

Thoughts of doubt hovered around me as Francisco said, "I, Francisco Alfredo Chavez, take you, Margarita Clotilde Ruiz, to be my wife."

"To have and to hold …"

"To love and to cherish …"

Daniel loved Belen, and she betrayed him with my Papa. What happened there? They had to have loved each other enough to have three children. So, where did her love go?

I wondered if Francisco would always feel butterflies in his stomach when he saw Margarita, the way he said he did. I couldn't imagine feeling that way about anyone.

"From this day forward …"

"Till death do us part."

Well, death did part Belen and Daniel. Maybe she departed when she fell for my papa. Romantic love doesn't seem real. Maybe it is mistaken for infatuation. I feel real love for my family. They are something to love and cherish. That kind of love will never die. I do not believe in romantic love, especially after hearing about Daniel and Belen.

Then something happened: something beautiful with brown hair and hazel eyes. Love became a young man who had been watching me for quite some time, laughing at my quizzical brow.

Chapter 10

Manuel Ibanez was a second cousin of the bride. He had come with his family from Elmendorf, Texas, just the night before. He was one of the youngest of eleven children, and he worked with his brothers and father in their small cement business.

He was nothing like the man I thought I would fall in love with. He was tall, very tall. He was not dark; in fact, he was quite pale with a little pink in his cheeks. He looked like someone who worked outside in the sun.

He was slim—maybe a little skinny for such a tall boy—and he had wavy, brown hair and hazel eyes.

I quickly looked away from his gaze and blushed. Luckily, the church was dark. I knew I was red as an apple and had no place to run away since we were stuck in the very front of the church. My leg began to jump up and down, and I crossed it over my other knee.

My mother put her hand on it to stop my fidgeting. "What is the matter with you?"

"Nothing." I kept myself from looking back in his direction and slowly began to breathe normally again.

The wedding was actually lovely. I was excited for my brother, but I still had so many things on my mind from the day before. Now there was this other distraction in the church. I could tell was still looking at me.

As soon as we were allowed to get up, I made my way back to our house and helped my family load the food onto the wagon. We needed to take it to the gazebo.

Elena said, "There will be plenty of boys for you to dance with, Rosa."

"What are you talking about?" I asked.

"My second cousins from Elmendorf are here," she said.

I had never been curious about boys until I noticed eleven brothers who took up a whole church pew, nicely dressed, and looking like they had just come out of a store catalog. He was one of them.

Elena said, "I saw of the Elmendorf boys looking at you."

I said, "Elena, I have so much work to do while we make the tortillas, and we have to do it outside on a comal heated by an open fire. I will not be able to socialize after smelling like a tortilla."

"I don't think one dance will hurt you. Come on! You're young and pretty. You need to start coming out of that shell of yours!"

I hadn't forgotten that we were cousins, but to me, she was still my big sister.

"Here, you can put this in your hair. I'll take care of your dance card," she said, trying to act like a regular American girl.

"We're doing dance cards?" I asked.

"Sure. It was Margarita's idea. That way, no one goes home without a dance to talk about. Have some champagne—it will kill your anxiety."

"I'm not anxious. I'm just worried I won't get these tortillas done. Look at all of these people. It looks like everyone who was invited actually came."

Tortilla after tortilla came right off the comal and onto our guests' plates. Mama and I were known for our tortillas. It didn't matter what meal we were preparing; there had to be plenty of tortillas.

As I prepared the soft, white flour or corn circles, the line kept bringing more and more people.

As I was about to take a break, the tall, lanky teenager with the hazel eyes flashed a smile at me, took the last tortilla from the hot black surface, and put it on his plate. "These are best, served warm," he said. His smile made the world stop moving.

The people behind him snapped at me to provide them with warm tortillas. The bean and rice line was not as congested, and I wished I had taken that job instead.

As the evening came to a close and people were slowly leaving the park, I had to begin picking up trash. I stood by a table of guests as they ate their last piece of cake, and then I swooped in like a vulture to take their trash so I wouldn't be the last person in the park at midnight.

Someone laughed from a distance as I gathered a spoon from the floor, wishing I were at home in my slippers and out of my dress.

The hazel-eyed boy knelt down and handed me the spoon before I could get it.

I dared not look at him, but I took it from his hand, making sure none of his skin touched mine. I walked away quickly without making eye contact.

"If you really wanted to help, you would grab a trash bag and gather more than a spoon," I said. *What is wrong with me?*

"I could do that if you danced with me first," he said.

I did have a dance card, and my sisters would never stop making fun of me if I came home empty-handed.

"And then you'll help me?" I asked.

"I would be my honor." He took my hand and walked me to the dance floor.

My hands were clammy, and I stepped on his foot as we began dancing, but as long as I pretended that he was my brother, I was fine.

"By the way, my name is Manuel," he said.

"Rosa. My name is Rosa," I said.

"You dance very well, Rosa," he said.

All those times I danced with my brother at my sister's weddings had finally paid off.

"So do you," I said.

The music changed, which let me know it was time to walk away.

"I'm supposed to help you with the trash now, right?" he asked.

"That was just a joke," I said.

"I wasn't joking. I'd love to help you." He grabbed a trash bag, smiled at me, and walked from table to table as I did the same. Every time I looked at him, he was looking at me.

At some point, I lost track of him and took my trash bag to the dumpster.

As I walked home with Jose, I said, "He reminded me of someone."

"Who did he remind you of?" he asked.

"There was this one boy who sat by me at a birthday party once. He did everything like a gentleman from the black-and-white films at the movie house. He had hazel eyes too. That was years ago."

When we reached home, I collapsed in my bed. I was exhausted from the wedding, but for some reason, I couldn't sleep.

Every Sunday, Papa would invite friends over for dinner after Mass. It was a good time for my sisters to socialize. I was glad to help out in the kitchen and stay away from boring conversations.

"May I help?" a strangely familiar voice said.

Mama gave him a large bowl of beans to take to the table.

He came back and took another large bowl of food to the dining room. "Anything else?"

My mother smiled. "Why are your cheeks red?"

"Why is he here?" I asked.

"Your father invited the family over for dinner. I thought you'd be happy. I saw you dancing with him at the wedding."

"Happy isn't the word. More like nauseated," I said.

"That sounds about right," she said.

Finally, Mother and I went to sit with everyone else and eat our semi-warm food.

Everyone ate and spoke about farming, children, and horses.

The boy turned to my mother and said, "At home in Elmendorf, my mother cooks bratwurst much like this chorizo. It would go well with your delicious tortillas."

She smiled again and looked at me.

I refused to listen to anything else he had to say. The stomach cramps came back.

"It helps if you drink seltzer water," said the green-eyed boy.

Oh my goodness! How dare he address me directly in front of my whole family? My face was burning. I grabbed the first empty bowl I could see, excused myself, and ran into the kitchen. I stepped out the back door and loosened my collar.

Mama soon followed. "What is the matter with you?"

"Why did Papa invite him?" I asked.

"Manuel?" Mama asked.

"Yes," I said.

"He's going to work with his father and the boys for a few months here in Celina. Why does he bother you so much?"

"He is very outspoken. He speaks like he's an adult, and he's only eighteen—or whatever. He's very arrogant."

"Well, he's very educated. You have to remember that they're a huge family with all of those boys! I couldn't imagine what that poor mother goes through to feed them all."

"He may be educated, but he's a show-off," I said.

"Well, he knows how to read and write, which reminds me. I was speaking to your father and he and I thought it would be a good idea if Manuel were your tutor."

I looked at Mama with shock and then quickly looked down out of respect, trying to remember my manners.

She said, "You don't look pleased. That's fine. You don't have to read. I never did, and I'm fine. Let's go back inside and finish our dinner."

We went back into the dining room, and everyone kept talking and eating. No one noticed we had come back into the room except for the green-eyed boy who stood up as soon as I returned.

Everyone stopped talking and looked at the hazel-eyed boy as he was looking at me and Mama. The other men looked at each other and slowly began standing up as well.

We weren't sure what to make of it, but Mama smiled with appreciation.

Mama and I sat, and everyone else watched the green-eyed boy as he followed. Then everyone sat down. I had never had so much attention on me in my life. It was embarrassing.

That night, I prayed my rosary in bed to keep my mind occupied with repetitive words. How I hated him in my thoughts.

I couldn't sleep. Ten rosaries later, still no sleep. All I could do was turn and twist in my bed. Then just as soon as I began to doze off, I heard the cock crow.

"Good morning, *mija*. Look at the beautiful day God has given us! Oh, dear! Do you feel all right?" Mama felt my face with her warm hand.

"Just give me the bucket." I headed out to the barn to milk our cow.

Mama followed. "Is there something on your mind?"

"No," I said.

"That's fine," she said.

"So, there's this boy who I hate. Well, hate is a strong word, but he makes me uncomfortable. At the table, he would just go on and on about our government and things that he'd read! That doesn't mean he's better than me. He cannot make tortillas like I do. He cannot sew or crochet the way I do. He can't have babies."

"Nope," said a voice.

I turned quickly to see the hazel-eyed boy standing in the doorway.

The sun came up behind his tall figure as I milked Helen.

"How long have you been standing there?" I snapped.

Mama said, "Did I tell you Manuel is staying in our barn? I have to feed the chickens."

This time, I won't be shy. This time, I will speak my peace. There is no one but Helen around to make me feel like I am being rude to our guest.

"Your mother tells me you might like to learn to read," he said.

Mama could read and write in Spanish. I didn't see what reading would do for a Mexican teenager who was going to be a wife and mother. I continued milking Helen.

"Well, if you want to learn, I would be happy to teach you," he said. "I could even teach you English."

"Why would I need English? We don't speak to the Americans. They don't speak to us. They just buy our food and go their way."

"All languages have their beauty. Listen to this." He recited something from *Two Gentleman of Verona,* which I learned later during our study of Shakespeare: "What light is light if Silvia not be there? What joy is joy is Silvia not been seen?" He said it in English—but with such tone and softness.

"What did that mean? What did you say?"

"It was part of a poem by William Shakespeare, meaning what good is light if the one you want to look at isn't there," he said.

I lost my grip on Helen's udder. She mooed and woke me from my trance.

"Here, let me show you," he said taking a worn-out book from his back pocket. He turned the pages and went straight to the sonnet that he knew by heart. The sounds were melodious, but I couldn't understand a single word. He pointed to the words as he read again, sitting next to me on the floor while I sat on my bench, next to Helen.

"What light is light …" He looked at me to repeat.

I knew the Spanish alphabet, which helped. "You didn't say this letter sound."

"The g is silent in this word. It's like a code. Every language has a code. Once you learn it, it becomes easy to solve. Here, say the words with me."

I moved my mouth like his and repeated the sounds he made. I spoke the English of William Shakespeare.

"Good," he said with a smile.

This time, I smiled back.

Chapter 11

The next day, I waited for our next class. I went from dreading the sight of him to anxiously wanting to see him.

That's how it was every day for the next few months. I was determined to master this thing called reading.

Jose was also learning to read.

I said, "Writing is so difficult. With Spanish, the sounds correspond to the letters. That isn't the case with English."

"I know. English is a Viking language—makes no sense at all."

"Manuel is so much older than me. Do you think he thinks I'm just a farm girl with messy hair and poor taste in clothes?"

"I don't know," Jose said.

"Girls his age are already perfect. They know how to put on makeup and how to smile at a man like Manuel."

"Maybe you should talk to Mom about this," Jose said.

"I want a man's perspective," I said.

"Well, he is a cool guy," Jose said.

I said, "He said he didn't have a girlfriend in Elmendorf, but I know he used to have one. She's probably still in love with him."

"If he were in love with her, he'd be with her," Jose said.

"He goes back to Elmendorf in three months. I bet she's pretty and has cute dresses. The only dress I have is the one from the wedding in which Manuel got to see me for the first time. At least I made a good first impression."

"He's coming," Jose said.

"Don't tell him anything I said."

Manuel pointed to his book of plays. "So, let's begin here, today. The best way to learn is to act out what we're saying to each other."

I said, "I love acting. That way, I can be someone else and not be an awkward, farm girl."

He said, "Exactly. It's not that you're awkward, but in theater, you can be a fairy queen from *A Midsummer Night's Dream*, and I can be your servant, Puck."

My hero was always Manuel. Three months, two weeks, four hours, and five minutes was all I had before he left, and I was going to make the best of it.

We acted every day in my parents' barn. My father thought I was learning to read and write, but he had no idea that I was acting out my innermost thoughts.

He said, "That was good, but next time, you need to stand right here. You need to whisper this line rather than yell across the barn at me." He placed his hand on my arm and led me closer to center stage.

I sighed.

"Are you all right?" he asked.

I was frozen. I could barely breathe. I felt my face turn hot. My palms began to sweat. I had never fainted before. *I can't faint.* "Yes." I took a deep breath, moved to my place, and lifted my head to say my line.

Manuel had found a Spanish translation, which I had been able to memorize better than the English version. Shakespeare probably hated it, but at the same time, he had to appreciate that his work was being recited and played out in a barn in Celina, Texas.

It was finally time to perform for my brother and his friends, and while they might not have understood all the poetry and double meanings, they were intrigued by the action that went along with the words.

Jose said, "Bravo, Rosa! I actually thought you were someone else. It almost looked like you were in love with the donkey!"

"My character *was* in love with the donkey," I said.

I tried reading everything I could find to impress Manuel. I read recipes in my mother's cookbook. I read the Bible.

Every now and then, Mama would get letters from Mexico. She never read them; she just put them in her pocket and took them to her room.

I told Manuel about her strange behavior. "She takes the letters to her room, but I never see her writing any back."

Manuel said, "I'm sure there's a perfectly good explanation for that. You know, we should begin a correspondence. I'll be going home soon, and I wouldn't mind helping you with your writing. That is … if you wanted to."

"You mean like pen pals?"

"Yes," Manuel said.

"What would we write about?"

It suddenly hit me hard. Manuel was leaving soon. He was leaving, and I would be left with nothing but an empty barn. The theater would be closed forever, and I would be left standing there doing soliloquies. My heart began to beat like a drum, and my vision began to blur. *He can't see me cry.* "I have to help Mama with dinner." I ran outside. I ran into the night and felt the rain pelting down upon my head. The rain blended with the tears streaming down my face.

He was behind me. "Rosa, where are you going?"

"I'll talk to you tomorrow!" I said.

I hoped he would stop chasing me—so he wouldn't see and so he wouldn't know the truth. I fell on the ground outside of the chicken coop and let my head rest on my knees. *God gave him to me for a little while, and now I have to let him go. I should have been grateful.* I knew I loved him, but I would never admit my weakness, especially since he was leaving me.

He came around the corner and said, "Why did you run away from me?" He was dripping wet.

I said, "I had to check on the chickens. The hen was fussy last night, and I wasn't sure if she would give us eggs in the morning."

Manuel took me by the hand since the mud had made it slippery below my feet. "Rosa, why did you really run away?" He wouldn't let go of my hand as he waited for my response.

I should have moved away. I was trapped by his gaze and unaware of my ability to breathe. His eyes looked bright green when the lightning flickered.

No one was speaking. The air around us had become thick and sweet like honey. I couldn't move.

He leaned toward me, making me dizzy, and I looked up at him. The rain felt warm.

"Why did you leave me?"

"I don't know," I said.

"I see." He moved closer, and then he stopped and backed away. "I won't bother you anymore."

I felt my whole body go limp. I leaned against the wall of the chicken coop and watched him walk away into the evening. I felt like I was stuck in a huge bucket of wet sand. I went inside, but my thoughts were still being tossed around in my head.

Mama came in with a towel. "Look at you. You're all wet. What's wrong?"

"I …" I wanted to tell her what was wrong, but I was tongue-tied.

"Are you all right?" she asked.

"I got wet in the rain," I said.

"What were you and Manuel talking about by the chicken coop?"

She had been watching? My face turned red again.

"We didn't do anything. He just stared at me," I said.

"Rosa," she said.

"He asked me about writing because I have trouble with writing."

"Writing?" Mama asked.

"And then he left," I said.

"He looked upset," she said.

"Yes. I think he thought he was bothering me— and so he left." I began to cry. *I don't want her to know that I am crazy in love with Manuel. I know love makes people crazy. Now she will be able to see how destroyed I am by the thought of Manuel leaving. He is gone—and who knows if he will ever come back! He thought he bothered me? I could have been with him for the last few weeks of his visit. I could have kept him close to me for a little while longer!*

"He didn't leave," Mama said. "He's in the living room with your father."

"What's he doing in the living room?" I asked.

"I think he's asking if he can court you." Mama smiled at me as if she knew all along—as if I was silly to worry.

"I never saw him come into the house," I said.

"He went to the barn to change his clothes since you two were standing in the rain for so long. What on earth did you do that for? You should have come in so I could make you a cup of hot coffee." She danced around my room, picking up wet clothes off the floor, and handed me a dry dress.

I whispered, "How do you know that's what they're talking about? They could be talking about horses or the business, or …"

"Rosa?" Papa said from the living room.

I ran into the room. "Yes?"

"Manuel will walk you to the store tomorrow." He looked at Mama, placed his arm around her waist, and gave her a smile. "He's a nice boy."

I didn't even know he liked me. He didn't even know I liked him—or so I thought.

The night might have gone quicker if I'd slept— and breakfast might have passed faster if I could eat. Minutes seemed longer, and the hands on the clock wouldn't move.

Finally, at noon, there was a knock at the door.

I wasn't ready. *My hair is a mess, my boots are muddy, and this is not the dress I wanted to wear.*

"Manuel." Papa shook Manuel's hand and led him to the living room.

"Good morning," Manuel said. "I came to escort Rosa to the grocery store—if that's all right with you."

He spoke with such formality that I almost let out a snicker.

"Call me Baldo, Manuel. Just because you're courting Rosa now doesn't mean we have to be so formal. Come in and have some lunch—and then you can take her to the store."

This was not like Papa. When my sisters dated, he usually had a knife in his hand, cutting an apple or a cucumber, when their boyfriends came over. *This is not like Papa.*

Mama hit me on the back of the head so that I could take the food to the table.

We ate in silence—except for Papa who discussed the matters of the day, the business, how his back hurt slightly from lifting, and how delicious the meal was.

When I stood up and began gathering the dishes, Mama took the plates from my hand and told me to get my purse. "It's time," she whispered.

I walked to my room, combed my hair back into a half ponytail, took off my apron, and looked in the mirror. I took a deep breath and walked out to the living room.

Manuel stood by the door and smiled at me. He opened the door for me, and I walked out. We walked to the road in silence.

He said, "I want to apologize to you for my behavior yesterday evening."

"That's fine," I said.

"It's just that …" He took a deep breath and looked around. "Rosa, I didn't know how to tell you that I had feelings for you."

I looked at the road ahead of us.

He said, "I didn't know how you would react if I told you how I felt—or if you would reject me or make fun of me. Even now, as I speak and you say nothing, I still wonder if you will have me … if you can see me as more than a tutor or an acting partner. I don't know what you're thinking sometimes. I mean, I think you like me because when we acted the parts of King Elizabeth and King Henry, it felt as if you were my wife, and that the only way I could be king was if you would be by my side."

My heart skipped a beat.

"Why did you run away?" he asked.

"I didn't want you to see my crying," I said.

"Why were you crying?"

"Because I didn't want you …"

"You didn't want me?"

"I didn't want you to go." I felt the tears again, but this time, I wasn't going to let them fall.

"I'm not leaving for a few weeks," he said.

"I know. And I knew it was going to happen, but it didn't seem real until we ended our play—and then there was nothing left to rehearse. I felt like the end of the play was the end of my life. Standing there on that stage with you, the barn, whatever, was the only place I wanted to be." It must have been the Shakespeare that gave me the courage to pour my heart out. Being honest had never felt so good. "When you started talking about writing to me, I couldn't breathe. I had to turn away and run so you wouldn't see me cry … so you wouldn't know how much I …" *I'm not supposed to say those three words. We haven't even finished our first walk during this newly formed courtship, and I am already about to proclaim my love.*

"How much you what?" he asked.

"I shouldn't say." I looked at him, hoping that would be enough.

"You can't say that you love me?" He led me to a large rock on the side of the road and motioned for me to sit down.

"I don't know what to say," I said.

He sat down beside me. "If you don't want to say it, because perhaps you are afraid of falling in love with someone who is leaving in a few weeks, I understand."

I remained silent.

"Rosa, tell me what you want."

It was a strange question. What I wanted was impossible. I wanted him to stay with me, but he already had plans to go to school. *What does it matter what I want?*

He placed his hand on my chin and guided my eyes to his.

When my eyes met his, there was no wall to hide behind. There was no chicken coop to run to, no kitchen in which to busy myself, and no play in which to act.

As he smiled, I took a breath. *He knows I love him.*

"I love you too," he whispered.

When he kissed me on my lips, it was clear that everything I wanted was him.

Chapter 12

How hard was it to say I love you to someone? Well, I say it to my kitty. I say it to Mama and Papa. "Mama, I love you," I said.

"I love you too, Rosa." Mama kissed my forehead.

I said, "The Bible spoke of love for God in the psalms, but I don't remember hearing any of the couples tell each other that they loved each other."

"What are you talking about, Rosa?"

"I know Jesus said, 'Love your neighbor as yourself,' but that's all I remember about the actual words."

Mama said, "You know, when I was young, I jumped in the water, feetfirst, when I saw your father swimming in the river. That's how he knew that I loved him."

"So, you didn't have to say the words?"

"Not at that moment—but they came naturally when the time was right," she said.

I said, "For the past two and a half months, I've thought of Manuel every day. Now that he said that he loves me, I'm afraid of thinking of him."

"Rosa, you're overthinking things," Mama said.

"Now that I have his love, I have to think about what I'm going to do with it, especially since he's leaving."

"Just enjoy your time together—while you can," Mama said.

"He's in love with me, but for how long?"

"So, would you rather he left and broke up with you?" Mama asked.

"No," I said.

Later that day, Manuel came to walk with me again.

I was so glad to see him, but in the back of my mind, I felt guarded. "Shouldn't you be with someone prettier, with nicer clothes, from the city, who already knows how to read and write?"

"What?" he said.

"Just saying," I said.

He kissed my hand. "I thought you were enjoying this beautiful day with me."

"You say you love me," I said.

"I say it because it's the truth," he said.

"Yes, but how do you know that when you go back to Elmendorf, you won't find someone who suits you better than a farm girl like me?"

"Rosa. Yes, I have known girls from where I come from who are what you describe, but I only want you."

I felt something getting warm inside my stomach—and slowly wanting to jump out of my throat. A little of me wanted to take those giggling girls and throw them down on the gravel and shove their fans down their throats. "Who are these girls? What are their names? How do you know them?" I felt the jealousy taking over like a raging fire flying around my head.

"That's all you heard? Rosa, I don't want anyone else," he said.

"I know how temptation works." I remembered my aunt's indiscretion.

"Look, I was supposed to go home with my brothers and spend the summer playing soccer, but I chose to stay and shovel dirt out of a pit in the middle of this town—because of you. When I found out you didn't know how to read, I went straight to your parents and asked them if I could tutor you and your brother. Everything went according to my plan." He smiled.

"So, ever since the wedding, you were planning to see me again?"

"You have no idea how beautiful you looked in that dress. I followed you the whole evening. I wanted to dance with you, but you were always working. I picked up a lot of garbage that night, but it was worth getting to dance with you."

"I was terrified of you," I said.

"I could see that. Do I scare you now?" He smiled again.

"Very much so," I said.

"Don't worry, Rosa. I'll be back. Can't you just enjoy this time we have together and not worry about tomorrow?"

"I worry about when you're gone," I said.

"When I return, we will be together—and it will be for good. We're going to write to each other, right?" He took my hands in his, ignoring the fact that they were cold and clammy.

I said, "If I write to you, you can't leave me hanging for days and days." I knew I was being needy and demanding, but I had nothing to lose at that point.

"I will write you as soon as I get your letter," he said.

"Will you tell me everything you do and send me poems from your book?"

"I will," he said.

"And will you deliver the last letter yourself when you come back to me?"

"I promise I will," he said.

"Then, I will hold you to your promise," I said.

It was easy to believe him at that moment, but once he was gone, I feared that the temptations of being away from each other would lead him astray—or lead him to forget me.

I found his first letter in the barn the day after he left. It was on the bed where he used to sleep. There was something absolutely lovely about his words written in ink on a single white paper. All of the little characteristics of his handwriting were etched in the threads of this treasure.

I smelled the paper and hoped to find his scent there. I imagined that he was actually talking to me as I read his letter.

Dear Rosa,

I'm writing to you, just as I promised. I haven't stopped thinking of you. My grandmother once told me something I want to believe. She said that when I think of someone I love, it's because they are thinking of me too. I hope this is true, my love.

Missing you,
Manuel

After doing my chores, I ran inside to my night table and pulled out a paper, hoping my penmanship would be lovely and sincere.

Dear Manuel,

Today I got up at the crack of dawn. I got out of bed, after having cried all night, and got ready to feed the pigs, gather the eggs, and milk the cow. The rest of the day, I read your letter about two thousand times, and now I have it memorized so that I can recite it like a soliloquy from Shakespeare. I can't go into the barn. It is empty like my heart. My words are simple. I wait anxiously to see your words in my hands again—if I can't see your face just yet.

Love,
Rosa
(There, I said it!)

Dear Rosa,

Today I worked with my father at his business. I did some correspondence for him and delivered some merchandise with my brothers. Soon, I will have enough money to come back and perhaps speak to your papa about something. Your letter made my heart break. While I am glad that you miss me, I can't stand to think of you any other way than laughing and talking about our summer together.

Just to correct you slightly: you did not say that you love me—you wrote it in your letter to me. Trust me, I will cherish these words forever, and I wait for the day when I actually hear your voice saying them to me.

Take care, my love.

Forever yours,
Manuel

Dear Manuel,

You must know that I adore you, but to say something so intimate is difficult for me and special at the same time. It will not be in the form of a scream, but in the form of a soft whisper: a whisper, close to your ear. Why don't you come here, and I will tell you how much I love you?

Yours,
Rosa

My Dearest Rosa,

How could you possibly know what you do to me when you tell me that you love me? I lie here at night in my bed with newly washed sheets, and all I can think about is that barn where the many smells and sounds of animals kept me awake some nights. I would rather have been there, knowing you would come every morning to milk the cow. Write me tomorrow. Tell me that you love me again—even if it's in print.

I love you,
Manuel

Dearest Manuel,

I love you, I love you, I love you.

Rosa

Chapter 13

We wrote to each other for five months. Whatever he experienced, I got to imagine through his words, and whatever I went through, he was able to do the same. Then, there were those times when I preferred not to read what he was doing.

Dear Rosa,

Today, I began my last semester of school. Science is interesting, but even though everything can be explained by science, there is still one thing that cannot be pinned down in an equation. Even though you are miles away, I feel a connection to you that surpasses time and space. Love is the opposite of science. I feel you by my side even though you are nowhere near me. I think of you when I read poems. I think of you when I go to church and sing the songs we sang together. I see the back of my classmate's head and notice she has long black hair like you. Everywhere I look, you are there.

Missing you,
Manuel

All I could read over and over again were those words: "my classmate's head." *Someone else had hair like mine?*

My beloved sent the letters without missing a day, and all I could think about was my sweet Manuel sitting behind a girl—a girl who was right there in front of him for at least forty-five minutes—who caught his attention.

I wanted to be the girl in class with him. I felt like a fool, thinking that this long-distance relationship could work out. This girl with the long black hair who shared an interest in science with him and lived in the same town as him would eventually take him from me. It felt inevitable.

Mama said, "You want to break up with Manuel?"

"Don't you see, Mama? Manuel and I are from different worlds. We love each other, but when he finds out that I know nothing about everything he's learning about, he'll grow bored of me. At least if I do it now, I'll look less like a fool than if I wait."

"Really?"

"Yes. I mean, don't you think I should look for someone like Papa, someone more like me. Someone who farms, you know … someone with a simpler life?"

"A simpler life?"

"Yes, you know. You and Papa were meant to be together—without a doubt. You live a happy, simple life here on the farm."

"Rosa?" She closed my bedroom door.

"Yes?"

She sat next to me and took a deep breath.

I knew I was wrong, but I wanted Mama to talk me out of it.

"I never told you everything about your father and what he went through when he was away from us. He has not had a simple life."

"You mean because of jail?"

"Your father was away from me for about a year, and unlike the two of you, we could never write to each other. It was torture for me, but he did what he had to do to come back to me."

I didn't realize that Papa had been listening to our conversation.

He said, "That's okay. Your mother told me that she told you I was in jail."

"I'm sorry, Papa. That's none of my business," I said.

"I suppose you're old enough to know the whole story," he said.

"You don't have to talk about this if you don't want to," I said.

"I heard you're worried about Manuel being so far away. If he really loves you, he'll come back," he said.

"Yes, Papa," I said.

Then he told me the story of his return to Mama.

"I was nineteen years old. I wasn't much older than you are now. I had a wife and two children, plus the children of my in-laws. I thought things were going okay, considering everything that happened by the river. But, like your mother told you, I had to leave. And, yes, I stole that bread. I was hungry and alone. Jail was actually a blessing. I had a place to sleep, free meals, and time to think. I even made a friend who was my guard. When my cousin came and paid to get me out, I thought I should come back to your mama, but I was a too proud. I should have come home right away, but I didn't want to come back broke. I went to work for a rancher."

The American rancher said, "You, there, what's your name? Do you speak English?"

"A little," answered Papa.

"Where did you come from?"

"I was released from jail two days ago."

"Are you a thief or murderer?"

"I stole a piece of bread," he said.

"No matter—we're looking for men who can work on the ranch." He handed Papa tools for gathering cotton and led him to the field.

Papa still had dreams of getting a house for Mama, overlooking the beach from a high cliff. He still believed in the American dream. Soon, he would go back to her with a little money in his pocket, and then they could continue living out their dream.

An older gentleman said, "Hold it like this—or your fingers will get blistered before noon!"

"Thanks." Papa extended his hand.

"You're welcome," said the man. "My name is Carlos."

"Nice to meet you, Carlos. My name is Baldomero, but you can call me Baldo."

"Welcome, Baldo. How is it a nice boy like you ended up in a place such as this?"

"It's a long story," Papa said.

"Ah. I see. Forgive me. It's none of my business."

"How did you end up here, Carlos?"

"About five months ago, my family and I decided to go to Colorado to find a job. You know, something better than in Mexico, where the rich got richer and the rest of us didn't."

"I agree," Papa said.

"My wife took a job working for a doctor."

"That's good," Papa said.

"Actually, she and the doctor began having an affair."

Papa wasn't sure how much he should pry.

Carlos said, "I'm Catholic. Even if I wasn't, I still love her. If, she decided to leave him for some reason, I would gladly take her back."

"I'm sorry she did that to you," Papa said.

"Is there someone you love? Do you have a woman?"

"Yes, I'm married, with two … five children." Papa looked down at the cotton.

"I'm sure you love all two or five of your children. I still hope to have a few of my own."

"I can tell you're a good person, Carlos. I'm sorry she betrayed you. That's the worst thing you can do to someone you love. I should know."

"Has she forgiven you?" asked Carlos.

"Who?"

"Your wife?"

"How did you know?"

"Wild guess … so why did you do it?"

"I don't know! To this day, I think of my wife: her smell, her taste, her long dark hair. I've never loved anyone else."

"Young love is the best," said Carlos.

Papa said, "I remember the first time I saw her. We were in church, and we kept laughing like kids do. My mother had to pinch my arm to make me stop."

"So, what happened? Who was this other woman who broke you apart?"

"My wife's sister," he said.

"Not good," said Carlos.

Papa said, "Don't get me wrong. She was beautiful, but I didn't love her. I love my wife. Here I am cutting branches, miles away from her, when I should be with her."

"Why aren't you?" asked Carlos.

"I need money for my family. I can't go back yet," Papa said.

"Can't or won't?" asked Carlos.

"I'm worried that my wife has had time to think and blames me for what happened to her sister," Papa said.

"What happened?" asked Carlos.

"Her sister's husband, Daniel, found out about us, killed her, and then killed himself."

"That's Daniel's fault—not yours," said Carlos.

"But I kissed her. How did I know that all this would happen because of a kiss?"

"Baldo, I've just met you, what, an hour ago? You don't seem like the type to want to ruin anyone's life— at least not on purpose. Did your wife forgive you?"

"Yes, she has been amazing to me," Papa said.

"Then go to her. Celina is only two days away. Forget about getting enough money. Stop making excuses for going to see her."

"Maybe she thinks I forgot about her."

"True love never forgets—and she knows that. Work here for a couple days. Make enough money to bring something to your wife and then go back to her."

So, after three more days of vigorous labor, Papa collected enough money and started on his way.

The rancher was hesitant to let him go, but he had no choice. "Have fun trying to get a better job anywhere else, Mexican!"

As Papa walked toward the gate, he yelled, "Carlos!"

"Baldo! I'm glad to see you going to your soul mate!"

"You should come with me." Papa took Carlos's hand and gave him a brotherly handshake.

Carlos said, "I should, but my soul mate is still here—and I want to make a little more cash."

"Are you sure?" Papa asked.

"As soon as I make enough money, I'll come visit you. Hopefully, by then, she'll see the error in her ways and come with me."

Papa said, "I'll be glad to meet her. You've been a good friend, Carlos. Thank you for everything!"

"Yes! Perhaps you'll see me sooner than you think! This heat is getting worse by the day."

"Until then, my friend!" Papa hugged Carlos. "Adios!"

"Adios!" said Carlos.

As the day grew to a close, Papa walked into the unknown, feeling uneasy, wishing his newest friend would forget about his cheating wife and come with him to Celina.

After a few miles, Papa decided to see if he could change Carlos's mind. It made more sense to walk with someone since the roads weren't always safe. He turned back and made his way toward the ranch, hoping he wouldn't be seen by the foreman.

He heard loud bangs being fired off in the distance. He wasn't sure if anyone could be hunting at that time. As he got closer, he heard more gunshots being fired and hid in the bushes. From a distance, he saw what could only be described as an assassination.

One by one, the men knelt down in the shadow of a large pecan tree.

The rancher and his partners shot the men, and they fell into the grave.

Papa couldn't see who had been murdered, but he wanted to make sure it wasn't Carlos.

He wanted to find his friend, but the bodies were buried almost immediately after they were killed. He would have died trying.

He ran away, feeling his heart race and knew that he would grow tired soon. The fear kept him going for miles, and he finally saw the lights of a town.

Should he tell the authorities about this massacre in his broken English? Would they believe a Mexican and his story of a reputable rancher killing several of his workers at gunpoint?

It was not the time to be a hero for men who were already dead. Papa knew he would find a way to avenge them someday. He didn't want to think his friend was one of them. Carlos was a strong worker. They wouldn't do that to him—he hoped.

Papa walked toward the lights in the distance for two days. As the second day of travel came to a close, he sat on the side of the street, hungry and tired.

In the distance, he saw a figure walking toward him with a basket of food. He didn't want to startle the girl, and he started walking in the opposite direction.

"Baldo," Mama said.

He froze at the sound of his name and felt tears fall from his eyes.

"Baldo!" Mama ran toward him.

They embraced and fell to the floor, feeling the familiar lines of one other's faces and snuggling against each other.

Mama kissed his hands, face, and lips. "Are you hurt? Come with me. Let's go home."

Papa held her tightly around her waist, not caring if his body ached.

She could barely breathe because his arms were wrapped around her so tightly.

"You are my home," Papa said.

Chapter 14

The next day, I sat with Mama on the porch, sorting fabric for a quilt. I thought about Papa's story all night. *Even though it took him a year, he came back to Mama. Will true love bring Manuel back?*

Mama said, "You have to have more faith, my dear. After everything your father told you, you still doubt that Manuel loves you? Manuel was telling you that he thinks about you all the time. What else could you ask for?"

"I guess I should ask for more faith." I took my letter and smoothed out its creases from my unhappy grip.

"Confidence is like sunshine to a flower. The more you give, the more it grows."

"Are you sure, Mama? Even though I'm here, and he's there—and he's surrounded by books and knowledge and interesting people with long black hair?"

"Don't you see? Even with all of these obstacles, Manuel still finds time to write you. He loves you." Mama kissed my head and tried to put my fears to rest.

As always, Mama was right.

Four months later, and nearly a hundred letters later, Manuel was at our table again—and the torture of my insecurities was finally over.

After he let Papa know of his intentions to marry me someday, he was allowed to walk me to the store every evening. It would take him one year to prove to my Father that he could support me, and then we would be allowed to marry.

"A year is a long time," I said.

"It's your father's wish," Manuel said.

"You know, Americans get married six months after they get engaged. Some of them even elope. I've seen it in the movies," I said.

"But 365 days will go by quickly," Manuel said. "I want to show your father that I can support my family. I'm going to start my own business. You'll see. I'll have my name right over the front door."

After a few weeks of searching for an office, Manuel began a painting business. He painted houses and small buildings. The wealthy ladies of the community noticed how crafty he was. They enjoyed his company and his ability to discuss politics and literature, and they kept him busy.

The money was good, and when he had enough to build our house, he took me to see the nearly finished home. "Do you like it?"

"It looks like the White House—except with four rooms instead of twenty. I like the kitchen and living room."

It had two lovely pecan trees on a large yard, a front porch up a flight of three stairs, and columns and a triangular portico design for the roof. He painted everything white and added black shutters to accent the windows. On each side of the windows, two red rosebushes were beginning to climb a trellis.

"I feel like the First Lady about to enter her new home," I said.

"I was hoping you would like it!"

The front porch overlooked the dirt pit in the middle of the town.

I said, "Can we grow some bushes so that we don't have to look at that?"

"I have that all planned out. We will plant tall bushes," he said, looking over our yard.

I smiled. "I see there's a room for our child."

"Yes, there is." He smiled too.

"Can you see us being parents one day?" I wondered if our child would be a son or daughter, if they would be tall like their father, and if they would have hazel eyes like him or brown eyes like me. "I can't wait anymore! I want to have a little mixed-up version of the two of us! I want to name them and show them off to all my brothers and sisters."

Jose walked into the empty house that he had helped Manuel build. "So, you've seen all our hard work?"

"Here are the fruits of our labors," Manuel said.

"Fruits?" Jose said.

"How are you, my brother that I never see?" I asked.

"I was at the house last Sunday," he said.

"I said, "You know you can come to dinner any day. We cook better than you wife does."

"She cooks just fine—and you forget I'm a newlywed. You'll find out what that means soon enough."

"True," Manuel said.

"Too bad you can't live here already," Jose said. "But you know what this place would be good for— now that it's all empty like this?"

"What?" I asked.

"A reception," he said.

"Hey, remember, the wedding scene from *Romeo and Juliet*?" Jose moved us around as if we were getting ready to say our vows in front of an altar. Somehow, he remembered all of the lines of the friar from the play, and then Manuel began to chime in. Before I knew it, we were reenacting a scene just before the wedding of Romeo and Juliet was to take place.

Manuel said, "Ah, Juliet, if the measure of thy joy be heap'd like mine, and that thy skill be more to blazon it, then sweeten with thy breath this neighbor air, and let rich music's tongue unfold the imagin'd happiness that both receive in either by this dear encounter." He took a ring out of his pocket, put it on my finger, kissed my cold hand, and placed it against his heart. "Will you marry me?"

I could only nod in affirmation as he lifted me off my feet and kissed my lips.

We ran home to tell my parents the news and write to Manuel's family. I wasted no time in writing down the details. I wasn't different from any girl who wanted to marry the man of her dreams.

I had a box of pictures I'd torn out of different magazines and samples of fabrics from my sisters' weddings.

It was finally my turn to prepare for *my* wedding. We would marry in the church where all of my brothers and sisters had done so. It was the same church where we were all baptized and confirmed. We would be on a stage—performing one of our greatest productions ever.

I had three sisters who had to pick their own bridesmaid dresses. Mama would have to play two parts. She would walk in as the mother of the bride and then be my matron of honor or *madrina*. Papa would give me away. I had been planning my wedding on my writing tablet, and without warning, I began to wet my paper with tears.

Manuel came to my side and said, "What? What did I do this time?"

I cried onto his lapel. "Papa is going to give me away!"

"Don't worry. He's not really giving you away. We're going to be at his house every Sunday."

"Yes, but here in the church, he will hand my hand over to you. I know I'm going to start crying."

"Rosa, that's perfectly understandable. It will be an emotional day."

"Why aren't you ever emotional? I'm a wreck!"

"I really don't know."

"I'll be right back," I ran to Mama and found her measuring the altar for the tablecloth she was making.

I heard footsteps behind me. Manuel said, "Rosa, where are you going?"

"I know! I know! I do love you—and I will marry you and be happy—but I need to talk to Mama for a minute."

"Look, if you and I are going to live as man and wife for the rest of our lives, you need to stop running away from me. Believe me when I say I will do everything I can to make you happy. Do you trust me?"

"I do," I said.

"Then stop worrying and marry me," he said, holding his neurotic bride-to-be in his arms.

A few months later, I married my prince. When he carried me over our threshold, about a hundred people were waiting for us in what would be our living room. Not everyone fit in the house, but we set up tables on the lawn.

It was lovely to be with our families. Manuel's family was there, and they were all so beautiful. All of his siblings had hazel eyes, and they were as tall and lovely as my husband.

My sisters were being nicer than usual. It seemed that I had finally joined their club of married women—and I would soon join their club of mothers.

Mama and Papa looked radiant as always, so proud of their last child, moving two blocks away.

After the last bit of meat was eaten and the last tortilla was tossed, we danced into the night to accordion and guitar, compliments of Manuel's brothers.

I hoped that my children would be just as talented and educated. Our children would go to the university—and I would do everything to make that happen.

Finally, after everyone had finished the last bottle of champagne, I began to clean my little house.

"No, not you," said Elida.

"The bride does not pick up the trash at her wedding," Elena said with a laugh.

"But I don't mind helping," I said.

"There's a car waiting for you out there," Elena said.

I quickly got up from bending over and noticed a long, black car.

"Ready?" With bags in hand, Manuel held out his arm to me and led me to the limo, which was driven by my brother. "Where to, sir?"

"You know where," Manuel said.

We drove for miles until I felt a little anxious. The Texas desert was lovely at night, but it never seemed to end.

When we reached our destination and the light of San Angelo, Jose opened the door and carried our bags to the front desk of a lovely hotel.

Manuel said, "Stand straight and proud, my love. Tonight, you own the place."

I pretended I was one of those starlets from the movies and had just arrived with my handsome leading man. I hadn't had time to change, and everyone congratulated us on our wedding.

After Manuel got the key to our room, we went up the elevator, which was a first for me. I never realized how modern everything was in the city compared to Celina.

Manuel carried me into our room, which was so lovely and white with light blue linens on the bed and crystal vases filled with red roses everywhere.

"It's just like a picture in the movies." I went into the bathroom to take a minute for myself, and I prayed to Our Lady of Guadalupe to calm my nerves.

On the balcony, we had a view of the city and the stars shining above us. In my husband's arms, I kissed him and said, "I love you."

Chapter 15

Our first child, Manuel II, was a splendid baby who arrived about nine months after the wedding. Our second, Viola, was a lovely girl who loved to wander around on her hands and knees, terrorizing her older brother. I thought two was perfect and more than we could handle, but the next year, Olivia surprised us. She ended up being a wonderful playmate for her older sister.

A couple years passed, and I was finally able to accomplish something in a day. I never knew that three little ones would bring me as much joy as they did sleepless nights.

Three was a good number, and we were happy. Then we became even happier with our fourth child, Jose Enrique. Most of his friends called him Jose, and he was tortured by his older sisters and loved by his older brother.

Manuel loved being a father.

We finally had enough money to buy a sofa, a dining room table, and a bed, which was where most of us slept.

Eventually, we bought another bed so that our oldest could sleep there. We needed to make room for our next girl: Katarina. The boys were beginning to notice that they were being outnumbered, but they made sure to take ownership of the extra room as they grew older.

After Katarina, I had Desdemona, who we called Desi, and she was the quietest baby. She hardly ever cried or made a fuss.

Finally, Juliet was born, and though the boys were hoping for another boy, we were so glad to have our sweet baby girl.

I never imagined I would have so many babies, and I marveled at how my body could actually go through this time and time again.

Going to church was always fun. I had the sweetest feeling as I looked over at all of my children in their finest church outfits. We sat in the middle of the church in case I needed to escape with one or two of them at any given time.

I enjoyed watching my children as they went to school, learned about dancing, and played sports. I went to every game and every performance without fail, and I brought along Mama to see how her precious grandchildren were doing.

Papa was an excellent grandfather. He taught our children how to farm and how to build things with their little hands. They never missed an opportunity to be with him.

Growing up in Celina wasn't always easy for me or my children. "Act as if you own the place," I said as they went off to school. It worked for me when Manuel said it, and I figured it would help my children too.

Viola found it most difficult to be insulted for being different.

I would say, "Remember, we are all God's children—even those who hurt you. He will deal with them when He decides."

Manuel said, "Education is the way to success, and with education comes respect." He wanted the best for his children, and there would be no question about it. His children were going to college.

Viola didn't care about finishing school and got married; she knew how to read and write and do mathematics. I was proud of her for trying, but love seemed more fulfilling than school.

My eldest joined the army as soon as he turned eighteen.

I brought in a box from the mail and said, "Look, he sent dishes from Germany!"

"What does his letter say?"

"He says he's met a nice German girl who he loves very much—and they're getting married!"

"Okay. I guess that's good news," Papa said, unsure of what it meant to marry a German girl since we were at war with Germany.

"He says they will be leaving Germany soon and are going to live in California. Oh, Manuel can we go to California?"

He could not resist making me happy. We visited soon after they bought a house there, and we took as much of the family as we could. Redwood Forest was a sight for sore eyes. It felt like I was in a cathedral of trees.

Manuelito asked, "So how is everyone?"

I said, "Well, your sister has nine kids now—and she lives in Abilene."

"Nine! How do they feed all of them?" he asked.

Manuel said, "Jose Enrique is going to college on a football scholarship. He was the salutatorian of his class, and his team went all the way to the state finals!"

"Good for him!" Manuel said. "I wish I could have seen him play."

I said, "I've been working at the hotel to help pay for tuition and extra expenses." It was the least I could do to help my son get through college, and it was worth every towel I had to fold.

Jose Enrique eventually graduated from St. Mary's University with a degree in physics. He was the only Hispanic in his graduating class. I beamed with pride, and my husband stood taller than ever before. On graduation day, the air force offered him a job. He took it without hesitation, having a new wife, a little boy, and a baby on the way.

My two younger girls were also in college, studying chemistry and nutrition. I was sure that they took after their father.

Juliet, my littlest girl, married young and stayed in town. Everyone else moved so far away. I wondered if it was me or the pit in front of our house. They said the jobs were better in the cities and promised to visit often.

For twenty years, it had been a whirlwind of activity with crying babies, first days of school, graduations, college trips, marriages, grandchildren, and so on. Suddenly, it was quiet—too quiet.

"What's wrong?" He sat tall and handsome, his hazel eyes hiding behind black-rimmed glasses. He had a little gray in his hair, but he was still the most beautiful thing I'd ever seen.

"Everything is perfect, don't you think?"

"What are you worrying about now?" he asked.

"Do you ever feel like there's something missing?"

"No—not as long as you're here," he said.

"I guess I just miss the chaos. I miss my babies and all of us stuck in a room together, crawling over each other at night to get to the bathroom."

"Really?"

"I miss going to church together and eating lunch after Mass. I miss Christmas with everyone here."

Manuel said, "Well, why don't we invite everyone for Christmas and do things like we used to?"

"It's so cold to travel, and the children will want a fireplace, which we don't have, you know for Santa?"

"Then we'll tell them to come Christmas Day—after Santa comes," he said with a smile.

"Do you think they'll come?"

"They'll come for Mama," he said sternly.

Chapter 16

Everyone lived so far away. I worried the whole time they were traveling. One thing was certain; I had everything ready for them. Carne guisada and tortillas were on the table, and everyone had a rollaway sofa or bed to sleep on.

Soon enough, I could hear the cars coming up our driveway. I ran outside to see my baby boy with his babies, and I opened my arms to see the most beautiful children dressed in their Christmas outfits.

Anna and Enrique Manuel hugged me. "Grandmother!"

"You see. They did miss you," Manuel said.

"Abuelo!" They loved being lifted by their tall grandfather.

"You're so big, Abuelo!" Anna said.

"And now so are you," he said, joking with her and keeping her in his arms.

"Don't carry her too much. She's going to get used to it," Celeste said. It was actually a blessing to have my daughter-in-law there to help me tidy things up a bit.

Christmas was fun but messy.

Mama also helped out by making her delicious tortillas. She had moved in with us after Papa died.

We thought he would be with us forever, but his heart gave out. His death hit all of us hard, especially Mama. She asked that his last words to her be carved on his tombstone: "You are my home."

Strangely enough, I never felt like he was gone.

From then on, Mama sat by the window in her rocking chair, knitting or praying. She had developed arthritis in her hands and feet. She also had trouble hearing with her right ear. Having her with me was such a comfort, and I cherished every moment I had with her.

"Abuelita Florecita!" Her great-granddaughter brought a teddy bear for Mama to play with.

"Ah mira el changuito!" Mama said. She loved hugging Anna's teddy bear, which she thought was a monkey.

"No, Abuela, it's a bear!" Anna repeated every time she visited.

Mama would forget—or perhaps it was just what she wanted the yellow bear to be.

Mama showed the photograph of her with Papa to Anna and Enrique Manuel so they could see what he looked like.

Anna said, "Wow! His face is so dark, and his hair so white!"

"Who does Abuelita Rosa look like?" Enrique Manuel asked.

"Well, she looked like me when she was little, but now she looks more like her papa." Mama walked over to her closet and brought out more mementos from her past. "This was the baby blanket Abuela Rosa had when we brought her to the United States." She let us feel the soft cloth and then placed it back in the box. "This belonged to your Abuelo Baldomero." Mama held a small Bible filled with pressed flowers and pictures of people from her past.

Anna said, "These are pretty flowers."

"He gave that to me a few months before he passed away. It used to be a red rose."

Enrique Manuel said, "You still have it?"

"He said he wanted me to keep it forever—to remind me of him." Mama put away her box and her memories.

I told my grandchildren to go to the living room. It was time to open presents. We watched, with anticipation, hoping they would love everything we gave them. Paper flew in the air, and their little faces gleamed with joy.

"Thank you, Abuelo and Abuelita!"

I got to enjoy their sweet embraces and felt the joy that only Christmas could bring.

The next morning, everyone else came for breakfast. The house was filled with my daughters, their grandchildren, and Jose Enrique's family. The children played outside, the men talked on the front porch, and the women gossiped.

We came inside and cooked for the day: tortillas and chorizo con huevos for breakfast, tortillas and carne guisada for lunch, and tortillas with honey for desert—after a huge barbecue dinner. We never left the kitchen.

We were so proud of Jose Enrique. I think my husband bragged to his friends every time they played cards that weekend. "Have you met my son—the engineer?"

Manuel came back from the mailbox and said, "Look! It's a response from the president of the United States."

"Of America?" I asked.

"Remember what your father said about his friend being killed by those ranchers?"

"Yes, but that was years ago," I said.

Manuel said, "Well, it may have happened years ago, but it never really stopped. After he told us that story, I did some research and found out through the newspapers at the library that bodies were found in the ground—shot to death in the same manner he described. The bodies had only been there for a few weeks."

I said, "You mean these ranchers had made a habit of killing Mexican immigrants for all these years— and they were never caught?"

Manuel said, "They had never been caught because the police tended to look the other way. It was the easiest way to get free labor."

"That's horrible," I said.

"I had to do something, Rosa. After all the letters and information I sent to the president, he finally answered me!"

He read the letter out loud for me to hear. I was in disbelief that our president had actually written back:

Dear Mr. Manuel Ibanez,

I cannot begin to tell you how it fills me with sorrow to know that your own father-in-law witnessed such tragedy.

Please know that I have not overlooked your letters to me, and while it has taken me much too long to answer you, your correspondence with me has not been in vain.

Action has been taken against these men who call themselves citizens of our country, but who I call criminals. They have been brought to justice, thanks to you and others who have made these crimes known to our administration. It was brave of you to take the initiative to write me, knowing full well that you were accusing men who once had great power due to their own greed and avarice.

Though many have been harmed due to these crimes, we are now keeping a closer eye on those who may have felt this was a common and acceptable practice, so that these acts will never again occur in our country.

Our Statue of Liberty did not say bring us your tired, your poor, and hungry, so that we could mistreat them. Our Constitution states that all men are created equally and should be treated as human beings.

With this in mind, I am personally writing to you to let you know of our actions against those who have wrongly used their liberty to hurt others. Thank you for your bravery to inform me of these events.

Most Sincerely Yours,
Lyndon B. Johnson,
President of the United States of America

I wasn't sure if Manuel realized how much this would have meant to Papa. He rarely brought up that horrible event, but I imagined Papa and Carlos were in heaven, happy to see that justice had been done. I was proud of my husband and all of his accomplishments. He was a man of his word.

One night, while we were in bed, Manuel said "We're going to Mexico." His face beamed with anticipation.

"How are we going to get the money to go to Mexico?" I asked.

"You always said you wanted to visit your homeland, right? Well, I was talking to Jose Enrique, and he can arrange the whole thing for us. I've been setting aside some money. Don't you think we deserve it?"

"We already went to California to see Manuelito and his family! That was an expensive trip!"

"Don't worry. We'll be fine. Also, this will give us an opportunity to get the paperwork we've needed for your Social Security check. You worked at that hotel long enough to get something back."

"What paperwork?"

"Your birth certificate, which we think is in the church where you were baptized."

"Can't they mail it?"

"Yes, but don't you want to see your homeland?"

"I was a baby. I don't remember anything about my homeland," I said.

"Also, the children want to come with us," he said.

"The children?"

"Yes! It can be like a family vacation."

I said, "Do you remember the trip to California with Jose Enrique, his family, and Mama? That was a lot to organize."

"Consider that a trial run. We made it didn't we?"

"Mexico?" *I had gone so far from home.* "I love you, Manuel."

"I love you too, but why do you say it now?"

"Because you still want to take me on romantic trips to Mexico," I said.

He pulled out a brochure. "You'll love it. Two weeks of sightseeing and—"

"Two weeks?"

"We'll need it for travel time," he said.

"Well, I've never been away from Mama for that long."

"She'll be fine. We'll have someone come and stay with her. Don't worry." He kissed me again, and then he turned off the light before I changed my mind.

Chapter 17

"You're going to Mexico?" Mama asked.

"Yes, Mama, but it's just for two weeks," I said, hoping she wouldn't be as shocked as I was.

"You don't know what it's like there. It's hot. You've never left me for this long!" She got up from the table to rinse her plate in the sink.

"You'll get to stay with Juliet and her family. The children will love having you!"

"Manuel wants your birth certificate?" Mama asked.

"Yes, for me to file for Social Security."

"How will the church be able to trust you to give you that information?"

"Well, with my ID and my passport," I said.

"Nothing says who you were before you were married," she said.

"I'm sure Manuel will think of something."

"I must go with you. You'll need me to help you."

"Mama, you can't travel with your arthritis and your hip. How will you be able to go up and down stairs and on the train? It will be uncomfortable for you."

"I must go with you—so that I can tell them that you are my daughter!"

I looked at her for a moment, not sure of what to say. The more she insisted, the more I had to think of ways to tell Manuel. "Of course, Mama. You should come with me. I would love to take you with us."

Her eyes filled with joy. She held my hand and then brought me to her so that she could hold me in her fragile arms. "Thank you," she said as she kissed my forehead.

"You're welcome, Mama." I left the room and walked into the bedroom.

Manuel had heard everything. Such was the life of living in a two-bedroom house with large vents.

"So, would that be all right with you, my love, who I love so very much?"

"If I hadn't heard the whole conversation, I would have said no," he said.

I wrapped my arms around his neck and kissed him on the cheek. "We'll have plenty of time to be alone together. I'm sure Mama has relatives she can spend time with while we go off on our own, right?"

"I'm fine with it. I'm just worried about her health. I'm going to have to take care of the both of you," he said. "Jose Enrique will be there—"

"Yes!" I said. "Jose Enrique and his family will help. Maybe the girls want to go too."

"Rosa?" Manuel seemed to realize that I had just invited the whole family to come on our vacation.

"Yes?"

"If we do this, it will be stressful," he said.

"And fun!" I said.

"It will take everything longer for us to stay together and travel and make sure all the bags are together and make sure no one gets sick from the water. We'll have to help your mother climb up and down the stairs."

"Speaking of my mother, I know she has kept in touch with her family over the years. There are bound to be addresses from her letters. I wonder if she wants to visit them—if they're still alive."

"I can't believe I'm agreeing to this," he said with a slight smile.

The next day, he called Jose Enrique and my daughters to see who could make the trip. When everyone had finished checking their schedules for the summer, eleven family members would be traveling to Tarandacuao.

Over the next few weeks, we shopped for things we would need for the long train ride, and Manuel and Jose Enrique figured out where we would go and how long we would have before getting to Tarandacuao.

I said, "Mama, I can't wait to see where you and Papa met—and where you lived as a young girl!" I gathered her things and began packing for our long trip.

"Yes." She smiled at the picture of her and Papa hanging on the wall.

"He must have been so handsome," I said,

"Yes, he was very handsome—and such a gentleman. He would have done anything for me," she said.

I said, "Mama, Manuel wants to know the address of your house in case you want to see who lives there now. I know you get letters from someone."

"Letters?"

"Yes."

"Ah, yes, just some correspondence I have with a nun there. Her family used to be friends with mine."

"Oh! Well, she must work at the church! How nice to already know someone so we can get my birth certificate."

Mama said, "Well, we'll see. She might not be there. She usually lives in Mexico City."

A few weeks later, Jose Enrique and his family came to visit for Manuel's birthday. It was a fine celebration with the whole family, lots of food, and children running around everywhere.

After everyone left, Celeste and Anna helped me clean the house.

Anna said, "Let's start in the bedroom—where all of you made a mess with your Barbies!"

Celeste said, "Why do you have so many dresses for this doll? I don't even have this many dresses for myself!"

Anna said, "She needs something for every season. These are the winter wardrobe, these are the spring collection, these are the fall fashions, and these are the summer swimsuits."

"What is this one doing under the bed?" asked Celeste.

"That's her blue nightgown," said Anna.

Celeste noticed an unopened letter under the bed. She noticed the address from a nun in Mexico dated a year ago. "Maybe your Daddy knows who this is from. It could be from the family in Mexico. Tell your Daddy to come in here."

In the backyard, some men were talking with Jose Enrique about his days playing high school football.

"Daddy," said Anna.

"Yes?"

"Mommy wants you in Abuelita's bedroom," she said.

"Okay. Tell her I'll be right there."

Anna said, "She said *now*, Daddy."

"Excuse me. I'll be right back."

Jose Enrique walked inside and said, "What are you doing on the floor?"

Celeste said, "There is a stack of unopened letters from Mexico."

"Let me see."

"Where did you find this? Were you snooping?" he asked.

"I was cleaning, and I saw them scattered under there," she said.

Jose Enrique looked closer and found a box filled with more unopened letters. "Look at all of these. Not one is opened. Why would Abuelita Florecita keep all of these and not read them?"

"Celeste said, "Does she know how to read? Maybe she was embarrassed to ask for help."

Enrique said, "She could have asked Mama to read them for her. I have to ask Dad. Wait here. Papa, can you come in here?"

"What is it?"

"We found these unopened letters from Tarandacuao."

Manuel said, "Let me see. I remember bringing in the mail, but I figured she read them."

I walked into Mama's room and said, "What are you all doing in here?"

"Rosa, come here," Manuel said.

"What?"

"Do you know why Mama never read any of these letters?"

"No, but I'm sure she has a good reason," I said.

As always, we had forgotten that the vent was right next to where she sat in the next room.

Mama said, "Why are they in my room?"

I said, "Mama, I'm so sorry. The little ones were playing Barbies, and while they were picking up their things, they found these letters."

She looked at the letters and then put them on the floor.

After a few moments, I said, "Did you need help reading them, Mama?"

"No."

"Can I ask who they are from?"

She said nothing.

I felt like I was prying.

"Do you have to know?" she asked.

"No, Mama, but we thought perhaps they could help us once we were in Tarandacuao."

"I am your mama." She began rubbing her eyes.

"Yes!" I felt horrible for intruding upon her privacy. I reached out to hug her and noticed her body beginning to tremble. "Manuel!"

Mama rarely cried. She had always been a pillar of strength under the most stressful situations.

"Mama Florecita, what's the matter?"

The rest of the family came around and stared as Mama cried in her rocking chair.

"My family!" she said through her tears.

I could do nothing but hold her hand.

Celeste said, "She's having trouble breathing! Call 911!"

I said, "Mama, what's the matter? What's wrong? Tell me what to do!"

All she did was sob and shake, never letting go of my hand.

The ambulance came, and I rode with her to the hospital, watching the technicians help her.

"She's having some kind of anxiety attack, but her heart seems fine. At her age, we need to get her stabilized," an EMT said.

I said, "Did you hear that, Mama? Your heart is fine. You just need to be calm! I'm sorry to have upset you! I'm so sorry."

After the doctor had a chance to examine her, he came to the waiting room. "She's fine, but she's asking for her daughter."

"Of course," I said.

"I'll come with you," Manuel said.

"Actually, she asked to speak to her daughter alone," the doctor said.

"She's probably just embarrassed." I walked with the doctor to Mama's room and saw her frail little body under the covers as she slept.

The doctor left us alone, and I shifted her blanket closer to her neck to keep her warm.

"*Mija*," Mama said.

"Mama, the doctor said you will be fine. You just had an anxiety attack. Just rest—and we can go home tomorrow." I fixed her pillow.

"I have to tell you something," Mama said.

"Why are you crying? What do you need to tell me?" I sat by her side and waited.

"What I have to tell you, I couldn't say before because I thought you would leave me."

"I would never leave you, Mama. You have been by my side through everything. Why would you say such a thing?"

"You have been my joy for all these years—since the day I first held you in my arms."

"Then why would you think I would leave you?"

"It was not me who gave you life," Mama said.

I thought she was being spiritual. "You mean because God gave me life?"

My confusion made her smile for the first time, and the room became lighter. She took a sip of water and looked at me calmly. "You are my daughter, and I love you very much."

"I love you too," I said.

"I'm going to tell you something I thought I would take to my grave," she said.

"I'm listening," I said.

Mama took a deep breath and said, "It happened sixty-five years ago in Tarandacuao."

Chapter 18

"Baldo!" Mama cried.

"What is it? Is it the baby? Is it time?" Papa asked.

"The baby is coming! Get the doctor!" Her baby was ready to come out of her. She had waited ten months for her son to come to the light. The storm made traveling dangerous, and she knew it would take longer for Papa to get to the doctor. The baby was coming fast. It wasn't like the first time when Jose was born. He took twenty-four hours and weighed nine pounds. Mama was excited to see her second son. She had a feeling it would be a boy.

She wanted another boy. She would name him Israel. He would be a little version of his brother.

Jose who was fast asleep, and she wondered if he should be moved to another room. The pain was coming faster and faster. Mama prayed.

After what seemed like an eternity, she heard the horses. She gripped the sheets to keep from screaming too loudly.

"Florecita!" Papa said.

"Take Jose out!" she said. "Doctor!"

The doctor washed his hands and rolled up his sleeves. "Don't worry, Florecita. You're doing fine. It seems to be coming fast. All we need to do is push."

Mama screamed louder and louder each time the pains came, and she wondered how much longer she would need to push.

Israel was a big boy—a strong boy—and after a few more pushes, he was out!

The doctor said, "You were right—it's a boy!"

"Give him to me!" Mama said with such joy in her heart. "Baldo!"

"It's a boy!" The doctor shook Baldo's hand as the happy father ran to his wife and child.

"Come in!" Mama smiled at his little face and cleaned him off little by little.

Papa said, "You were right! He's huge! Look at those arms and cheeks!"

"Israel," Mama whispered.

"Israel," Papa said.

"He's beautiful," Mama said.

Papa kissed Mama on the forehead.

That night, all three of them slept together. Papa wrapped his arms around Mama, and Mama held their baby. She watched over him as he gently breathed on her arm, and she kissed his soft skin every time he moved.

The next morning, Mama began to feed Israel. He drank a little bit of milk and then stopped. For a few days, he seemed less and less interested in drinking from his mother and slept more than anything.

After a few weeks, Mama and Papa decided to have Israel baptized.

The doctor came to the baptism and noticed that the baby was losing weight.

"Doctor, he's not drinking as much as he used to," she said.

"Give him time," the doctor said.

Mama never left his side. He slept more and more, but she never gave up hope that he would soon begin to eat more.

Her breasts were full of milk, and she needed to feed him, but he would not drink from her. The more he slept, the less he ate. One day, as he slept in Mama's arms, he didn't wake up.

There was a funeral Mass a few days after the baptism. Mama was in mourning for several days.

People brought food for the family, and everyone tried to help the family in any way they could.

"Florecita?" Papa was afraid to speak to his fragile, young wife.

She had not said a word since Israel died. She looked in his direction but not quite at him.

Papa brought her a bowl of soup "Florecita, you have to eat something."

As she looked down at the bowl, she noticed her dress was soaked in breast milk. She turned her head away, feeling the desire to feed her child. He was gone, and she still had milk for him—milk he would never drink.

"Here, let's get you a new dress to put on," Papa said.

Belen said, "Florecita?"

Mama didn't pay attention to her.

Belen said, "Florecita, let me help you get into your dress and out of this one. You know, like when we were little, and I used to dress you up?"

"Go to your children, Belen," Mama said. It was the first time she had spoken in days. "Where is Jose?"

"I'll get him for you," Papa said.

A few moments later, Papa brought in a handsome baby boy, not yet two years old, who had been sleeping in the next room.

"My Jose." Mama held him in her arms and rocked him for as long as she could stay awake.

Chapter 19

Not far from where they lived, Mama heard of a family who needed assistance with their newborn child and their three-year-old baby girl.

The priest thought it would be a good idea to give Mama something to keep her mind occupied after losing Israel. Her depression had gotten worse over the past few days. She had no desire to bathe or cook, and she was neglecting everything and everyone except for Jose. She clung to Jose as if he were all she wanted to live for.

At the same time, she was still lactating. The discomfort in her chest was a constant reminder of her dead baby. She had healed well after giving birth and felt the need to be out of the house where her baby had died. She agreed to help at Anita Cerrano's house for a few days.

Anita said, "Thank you for coming to help me, Flor. I haven't been able to get out of this bed, and there's so much to do."

Anita's daughter said, "Mama?"

"Come here, Lorena!" said Anita.

Mama said, "What a pretty girl. Jose will love playing with her. I have a little boy. He's about her age."

Anita said, "Well, this will be perfect. I was worried about leaving Lorena alone in the house, and now she'll have you and a playmate to watch her. It's just until I can get out of bed. Thank you, again, for coming."

Papa could see the difference in Mama's personality. She came home every night after finishing the dishes at the Cerrano house, feeling more like herself and talking about the baby every chance she could get.

"I never knew how sweet little girls could be. You should see how Lorena plays with the baby. They are so adorable. Baldo, as soon as we can, we need to have a baby girl. Can we try again, soon?"

Papa said, "Of course—anything to make you happy. We can have as many babies as you want. Maybe a little girl and then a little boy!"

After the tragedy of losing Israel, Papa was excited to see Mama ready to continue their family.

Mama said, "I wish we could have a baby tomorrow! This milk is driving me crazy!" Her breast milk had stained many of her blouses.

Papa said, "First, you need to heal completely, and then the doctor said we can try again."

The next day, Mama went to the Cerrano house and noticed the doctor had been by. Things didn't seem

quite right with Anita, and her husband was still away,
working at the silver mines.

Mama went into Anita's room to bring her dinner
and found her crying.

"Florecita," said Anita.

"Yes, do you need something Anita?"

"Come sit by me." Anita was a beautiful young
woman with long black hair and light brown eyes.
Her skin was fair and flawless, like a shiny pearl. She
was one of the most beautiful women Mama had ever
seen, and she instantly grew to love her as a friend.
"I've seen you with my daughters. Lorena likes you
very much. How old are you?"

"I'm turning sixteen soon," Mama said.

"I'm eighteen," said Anita. "I noticed … I hope you
don't mind me saying, but your blouse is wet."

Mama quickly looked down to wipe her blouse.

"I noticed the other day that you are still lactating."

"Yes," Mama said, quite embarrassed.

"Florecita, there's something I need to ask you."

"What is it?" Mama asked.

"If I die, will you take care of my babies?"

"What are you talking about, Anita? You're fine!
Why would you say such a thing? Don't talk like that."

"My husband has not returned, and he has written
me several times. The roads are still very difficult to
travel on. I'm just worried about who will watch over
my children if he does not return in time."

"I'm here to take care of you."

Anita said, "I know. You have been so good to us. Please say you'll watch over my girls."

Mama looked at Anita, not sure what to say. "I will," Mama said.

As the days went on, Anita became less and less able to feed her baby.

One night, while carrying Rosario in her arms, Mama looked at Anita—who was smiling at her—and she knew what she was asking her to do.

"Thank you," said Anita.

Mama sat next to Anita, unbuttoned her blouse, and gave Rosario milk.

Anita lived a few more days—just in time to see her husband one more time. He arrived during a terrible storm and held her in his arms, along with Lorena, who was to ready to say goodbye to her mommy. The next morning, Anita passed away.

Mama ran home to be with her own husband and hold Jose.

Papa was unable to calm her. "Please stop crying, my love!"

"I love you so much, Baldo. Promise me you'll never die, you'll never leave me, you'll never leave my side. Just don't ever leave my side! Promise me!"

Papa held her and said, "I promise. I will never leave you. Shh. *Te lo prometon.*"

"She died," Mama said. "That beautiful girl died!"

Papa said, "I'm so sorry, Florecita. I had no idea she was so sick."

"She held on until she could say goodbye to her husband, and then she died this morning."

Papa said, "That poor man ... he has two daughters and no one to help him."

A baby cried.

Mama said, "Rosario!"

Papa sat up. "You brought the baby with you?"

"I had to! The doctor told me to. He knows that I feed her, and he took the other baby with him for his wife to care for her." Mama took the crying baby in her arms and let her eat.

Papa said, "Flor, we can't keep this baby here!"

"Anita asked me to feed her. I have no choice."

"What about our plans?"

"They'll have to wait."

Papa said, "I wanted to tell you this yesterday, but you weren't here. Daniel wants me to travel with him to California ... next week."

"Why now?"

"The gold rush is happening now, Florecita. We have to take advantage of this opportunity."

"Can't you see I need you? I can't take care of this baby and Jose alone!"

Papa said, "You'll have to find someone else to take care of the baby. It will be too much for you."

"There's no one who can feed her. I thought you would be leaving in the spring!"

"I thought so too, but he changed his mind. Florecita, I promise to come back as soon as I can—and then I will help you with the children. Until then, we need to tell Mr. Cerrano that this is too much responsibility for you!"

Mama said, "Are you crazy? He just lost his wife a few hours ago! She asked me to take care of them, and I said I would!"

"She belongs with her father, Florecita," Papa said.

Mama looked down at the baby in her arms and smiled at her, feeling the warmth of this little girl who lived because of her milk, because of a promise she had made to her mother, and because of the genuine love she had for Rosario. "She'll die without me. I know she is not mine, but her mother left her in my keeping."

A few days later, the doctor came to check on Rosario. He saw the luggage by the side of the door and heard Mama and Papa arguing.

Papa said, "You don't have to go, Florecita. I'll be coming back in a few weeks."

Mama said, "How can I stay here by myself? My sister is going with you and Daniel. I want to go with you too. I want to get away from all these sad memories."

"Florecita, Rosario will die without you," the doctor said.

Mama looked at Papa. "I need to be with my husband. I can't stay here and think of my son's death. Couldn't I …"

"What?" Papa asked.

She picked up the baby "Couldn't I take her with me?"

"That's not possible," Papa said.

The doctor said, "You say you're coming back in a few weeks?"

"Yes! I'll bring her back!" Mama said.

The room remained silent for a moment.

"Are you sure you're coming back?" asked the doctor.

Mama said, "Yes, in a few weeks. We promised my parents we would we would be back."

The doctor said, "Then I will tell Juan Carlos about our decision. He will not be pleased, but it's what's best for Rosario. Perhaps he can arrange to go with you. We'll see. Besides you're coming back."

Everyone agreed that it would be a temporary solution. It seemed like the perfect plan.

I sat in the hospital room, waiting for more, but Mama stopped speaking. She had finished her story.

A silence thickened the room like dough expanding from corner to corner in a pan.

I was not ready to hear what she had to say next.

"Your real name is Rosario," Mama said. "Rosario Cerrano."

Chapter 20

Nothing could have pulled me away from Mama, but she thought I would leave her if I knew the truth? At her ripe, old age and in a hospital room, where she thought she might be dying, she figured she had nothing to lose. "Now you know," she said.

Manuel came back into the room and found me shaken and unable to speak. He asked the doctor to check my blood pressure.

They gave me some medicine, and then Mama began to grow anxious.

The doctor wanted to separate us.

"Mama, are you all right?" I asked.

"You still call me Mama?" she asked, reaching for my hand.

"Well, yes. That is who you are."

"I'm sorry for keeping this from you for so long. I meant to tell you, but the years kept flying by—and I couldn't think of losing my family."

"No, Mama. We're never leaving you!"

They gave Mama a sedative, and she went to sleep. I held her hand and never left her side.

After the shock wore off, I began to put together the pieces of my childhood. *No wonder I never looked like my brother. No wonder I didn't look like anyone in my family. The woman who I thought was my birth mother was not, but she loved me as if I were her own.*

The next day, Mama was feeling better. We went home and began searching through the letters for more information.

My son brought boxes of unopened letters from my mother's trunk in the shed. With Mama's permission, Manuel and I read about people in Mexico who I'd never heard of.

Somewhere in Mexico, I had a sister named Lorena. I had a father named Juan Carlos. He was no longer alive, but he had asked about me in his letters. *How he must have suffered, not knowing what happened to me. I wish I could have met him.*

I said, "Manuel, God is sending me to Mexico to find my family. I have a sister I've never met."

Mama said, "This one is from Petra. She lived with the priest who visited your father from time to time. She kept asking when we'd be back. I never knew what to say … so I stopped answering."

I looked at a letter from a year ago. "Who is this person?"

Mama said, "That is your niece. She is a nun who works in the convent as a Mother Superior. I started receiving letters from her. She was very polite but persistent. The letters kept coming. I guess I thought you would find them after I died."

"Mama, no matter what, we are family—and we're still going to Mexico. It's time to see our home, Mama!"

Neither of us had been back in more than sixty-five years.

"Do you think they will hate me?" she asked.

"How could they hate the woman who saved my life?" I asked.

We left for Mexico a few days later, after arranging for everyone's passports, hotel arrangements, and train tickets.

I let my husband and son take care of the details. My mind was definitely elsewhere. It was somewhere between imagination and uncertainty. I had no pictures of my family and no way of knowing what they were like. I wondered what the town was like where I was born and if my Mama would like to visit her old house.

Sixty-five years is a long time. I had a sister. I was still trying to get my head around all of this after reading every last letter.

Mama was calm throughout most of the trip, praying her rosary and hoping the family didn't resent the fact that she took me from my family when I was a baby. We all knew it was out of necessity and love. She thought they would think that she was selfish for not telling me about my true identity and family earlier, but as far as I was concerned, she and Papa gave me a wonderful life.

The train passed through little towns and large cities, and I felt safe leaning against Manuel with Mama near me.

I said, "Manuel, do you think she'll be excited to see me?"

"Your sister?"

"My sister ... Lorena."

"Don't worry. She'll love you. We're supposed to meet Sister Celia, and she will take us to her. The only problem is that she might not be able to meet us there right away. So, we'll just wait ... and maybe get something to eat."

"Wait?" I asked.

"You've waited sixty-five years—what's a few more hours?"

"A haven't waited sixty-five years. I just found out about her the other day. I mean it's not like she's some long distant cousin. She's my sister!"

Manuel said, "If Sister Celia takes too long, we can ask around."

We got off the train and rented cars, and everyone gathered their luggage into the two vehicles.

I watched Jose Enrique's children playing together while we were on the train. They were the same age difference as my sister and me.

We arrived in the little town square of Tarandacuao, Guanajuato, just in time to have dinner and then rest on park benches. The park was across from the church in the plaza, which was where my birth certificate might be.

I sat under a tree, resting my tired ankles.

There was no sign of Sister Celia.

Manuel said, "Do you want some mango?"

"Mama, do you want some mango?" I asked.

"Yes," she said.

"Let me go to the fruit stand," Manuel said.

He and Jose walked to the fruit stand while, the rest of us laughed about our journey and its adventures so far. Two of us had thrown up on the side of the road from car sickness on the winding roads. Someone else fell off the stairs of the train while getting off, and we got caught in a surprise rainstorm one night. Luckily, we ended up at a motel near a beautiful lake with bougainvillea in full bloom. I was hoping we could go back there with my sister.

A few minutes later, Manuel came back with my mango on a stick. It tasted as sweet as ice cream. I was enjoying my fruit so much that I didn't notice my husband and son huddling with the rest of the family and discussing something I wasn't meant to hear.

I said, "Mama, have you ever tasted mangos this delicious?"

"Yes. You forget I used to live here," she said as she bit into her mango.

Manuel said, "Are you ready?"

I was ready to take a bath and get to bed. "Yes," I said as I got my purse.

We got into the car and drove for a good distance. When the pavement ended, there was nothing but a dirt road.

Eventually we came to a small adobe home on a ranch. There were hills all around and tall trees on the land. A goat and some chickens welcomed us.

"Where are we?" I asked.

Manuel said, "I thought you would go crazy—so I decided not to tell you right away."

My children smiled at me. I wondered if this was where the nun lived. Perhaps we were at the first step on our way to finding my sister.

A little lady in black and white came out of the house, held her hands out to me, and embraced me. "Tia! We have been waiting for you for quite some time." Tears welled up in her eyes.

I wasn't sure how to react. Something about her smile was familiar. "Sister Celia?"

"Yes, please wait here," she said.

"Why can't we go into the convent?" I asked.

She entered the red adobe house with roses sprawling around the front. In the courtyard, I could see a woman with gray hair in a small bun, peeking through the window with another lady by her side.

A few moments later, she came running out of the house. She came closer to me and placed her hands on my cheeks. She touched my white curls of hair and smiled. Her eyes were the same color as mine. She wrapped her arms around me and said, *"Hermana!"*

She called me sister! I can barely remember the rest. All I could feel was the weight of her body bringing me down to the ground.

"Lorena," I said.

The next thing I knew, we were being led into the house by my husband and son. My sister had fainted and taken me down with her. She was crying and laughing at the same time. I was crying and worried about her.

Sister Celia said, "Bring them into the living room. Come, Mama, let me get you some water."

There were so many people around us, but all I could see was my sister. I could see the similarities between us, and her smile warmed my heart like no one ever had.

After we recovered from the shock of seeing each other for the first time in sixty-five years, we talked.

We sat up for hours, drinking coffee and tortillas with honey, until the cock began to sing its morning song.

My sister told me tales of my past and of life growing up in my hometown. "I missed you," she said as she held my hand. She was so lively and cheerful; it was difficult not to love her.

We talked about our children, our husbands, and my parents—and what they looked like.

"You look like her," she said, pointing to a picture on the wall of a married couple. My mother was beautiful. She had jet-black hair, full lips, and an oval face like mine.

My father was handsome and had a gentle strength about him. He also had dark hair, dark eyes, and fair skin. I felt so bad for him, thinking of what he must have gone through after losing his wife and baby. I wanted to know all about them.

Mama had been sleeping the whole time in the other bedroom—or so I thought. We went in to check on her since I knew it had been difficult for her to experience so quickly and without warning. "Mama," I said.

She was praying her rosary.

A woman walked in and said, "I am Lorena. You took care of me a long time ago. Do you remember?"

"You were very little then," Mama said.

Lorena said, "I wanted you to know that I am grateful to you for watching over my sister all these years."

"You must hate me," Mama said.

"No. God knows why things happened the way they did. I'm just glad she's back. All those years with so many secrets in her heart. It's no wonder she spends her days praying that rosary."

As we walked to the kitchen. I said, "Please know that she had every intention of bringing me back."

"All is forgiven, Rosario. We know what happened. She wrote to a friend of ours many years ago about her sister and husband and about her love for you. Though I felt a longing to have you close to me, I was content to know that you were safe and loved. I just wish I could have known you sooner."

"Me too," I said.

Lorena said, "I know. I wish I had known you all my life. I wondered if you had gotten married or had children. I used to play with your baby hands and wrap your fingers around my thumb. I slept with your blanket and pretended it was you."

"I don't know what to say. My mother did what she did for very good reasons. She saved my life, and I'm thankful to her for that."

"So am I." She took a sip of coffee, added some honey to a tortilla, and gave it to me. "Here we are, two old sisters sitting next to each, as God intended. We have so much to talk about." She giggled like a schoolgirl.

Chapter 21

I looked at my sister's hand, wrinkled from working under the sun, making a million meals, and washing her babies and grandchildren. I took my fingers and wrapped them around her thumb.

Manuel decided we could extend our visit for a few more days to give us a chance to get to know each other better. He stopped and smiled at me. "I'm glad you're happy."

As he closed the door behind him, my sister smiled at me and said, "How did you meet him?"

I sighed at the thought of those first days of love when all I could think about was how I would be able to see Manuel again. He was so handsome, so intelligent, and so well-spoken.

"Oh, my goodness. It's been so long since I thought about that day," I said.

"So, how did he catch your eye?"

I felt like a schoolgirl sharing secrets in the girls' bathroom.

"He was tall, and he had these hazel eyes." I looked at the door, hoping no one was listening.

"Was it love at first sight?" asked Lorena.

"More like terror," I said with a laugh.

"What? Why?" asked Lorena.

"We were at my sister's wedding. I had never felt so sick in my life. I had butterflies in my stomach when he looked at me. And you?"

"That's it? There's more to that story," she said.

"How did you know Alejandro was the one?" I asked.

"I think it was, and I know this sounds bad, but I think it was how he smelled." She took a deep breath as if she could remember his scent. "I was a little girl at a candy store, walking around, and this boy ran right past me. He knocked all of the candy out of my hand. I picked up my *obleas,* and he helped me. I could smell something like fresh grass and soap. My world stopped for a few seconds. So, you were at a wedding?"

I took a deep breath, never having been asked about such intimate details before. "I was picking up trash from the floor at my sister's wedding. I kept tripping over my bridesmaid dress. It was terrible. A tall, skinny boy offered to help me. Then he asked me to dance."

"Isn't it funny? We both met our husbands while picking something up off the floor!"

I hadn't laughed so hard in a long time. I had tears in the corners of my eyes, and my stomach hurt.

The door flew open and Alejandro said, "What on earth is going on in here? What's gotten into you two?"

"Nothing," we said in unison as we began laughing even harder.

Manuel said, "We were thinking of making barbecue so that you two won't have to cook."

Alejandro smiled. "Except for the tortillas."

Lorena said, "Of course."

"Shall we?" I took my sister by the hand.

We had noticed that we had two things in common: the way we met our husbands and the fact that neither of them could make tortillas.

I said, "Why don't you make them? I'll help form and flip. I'd like to see how you do it."

"I take flour, lard, water, a pinch of salt and sugar, and mix it all up," she said.

"You add sugar?" I asked as she worked the dough in her hands.

She looked at me and said, "Well, yes. What's wrong?"

"Who taught you to add a sugar?" I asked.

"Our mama," she said.

The only noise we made after that was the sound of the water drops on the hot comal and the slapping of tortillas in my hand. It was a tribute to our mother. She had taught us how to make tortillas—even in different parts of the world.

Later that evening, after barbecue, beans, corn, and tortillas, my sister and I sat outside and drank black coffee with lots of sugar.

"Tell me more about my mother," I said, picturing the beautiful woman with black hair, who would never grow old.

"I'll tell you about the first time she showed you to me," she said. "I remember walking into the bedroom. She looked tired but so happy to see you. She played with your fingers and your toes, and she combed your thick black hair. She just kept smiling at you and at me, singing the song of the little trees that looked like twins: *Dos Arbolitos que parecen gemelos.*"

"The children are coming back from their walk," I said.

"Hello, ladies," Manuel said.

"She told me how you two met," said Lorena.

"Did she?"

"Did she tell you how we met?" asked Alejandro.

Lorena smiled.

Alejandro said, "Did she tell you that I made her drop her candies so I could have an excuse to talk to her?"

"Is that why you ran into me?" she asked.

"Did she tell you that I dropped trash near me so that I could pretend to help her?"

"You dropped trash on the floor?"

"Someone had to make the magic happen!"

I blushed—thankful that no one could see me under the night sky.

Chapter 22

After many long goodbyes and hugs, I left my sister and her little ranch in Mexico. It broke my heart to leave behind what I had just found. I promised to write her, and we made a pact to keep in touch. I wasn't sure if I would ever see her again.

It was good to be home among my things and my family, but every now and then, I would sneak a phone call to my sister.

"Rosa, have you seen the phone bill?" Manuel asked.

"Those phone companies!" I said.

"I understand you're still getting to know your sister, but … I mean, I suppose it's worth the money."

"I wish they could come here. It would be an exhausting trip to say the least. I needed at least two days of rest after our trip. But letter writing is fine."

That summer, Manuelito invited us to visit him in California. I loved California. The climate was cooler, and the ocean views were spectacular. The Redwood Forest was amazing to drive though. I actually drove through a tree trunk.

When we arrived at my son's house, he prepared a lovely meal and set up a picnic table in his backyard.

"Nice sunset," Manuel said.

Manuel and I stayed outside after dinner to listen to the creek behind the garden.

I said, "It's so beautiful here. I don't think I want to go back to Celina. This is much prettier than the hole in the ground."

Manuel said, "I wish our soil could grow lemon trees!"

"I could listen to that creek every night! It reminds me of when Lorena took me to the Ojo de Dios. It looked like paradise."

"El Ojo de Dios: The Eye of God. I sometimes wonder why God let you ladies stay separated for so long, while He watched from above."

I said, "I don't know, but I never would have met you if I hadn't come to Texas."

"Very true," Manuel said.

"Anyway, He brought us back together in his own time," I said.

"Yes, He did."

"I think I'll go write my sister and tell her about Manuelito's garden," I said.

"Why don't you tell her when you see her."

"Who knows when I'll see her again?"

"I guess you're right." Manuel held my hand.

I said, "You love California, don't you?"

"I do. Isn't it funny that you were supposed to come here when you were a baby and never quite made it, until now?"

"That's because my son lives here," I said.

"And you love to travel," he said.

"I love to travel with you. I love falling asleep on your shoulder and waking up at our next destination."

"Then how about we take another trip?"

"We're already on a trip."

"What about a trip to see your sister again?"

"From here?"

"Yes," he said.

"But I don't have enough clothes. The house will be left for so long! What about Mama and my plants!"

"Don't worry. I took care of everything. Jaime and his family will watch the house and water your plants, and all your clothes have been washed so you have a whole wardrobe to make the trip. It will only be for a few days, and there's someone to watch Mama. What do you say?"

"Why didn't you just ask me if I wanted to go to Mexico? I would have said yes."

He led me to the creek behind the lemon trees. "That would have ruined the surprise!"

"I don't need any more surprises. I'm old! Just tell me what we're doing next time so that I can be prepared."

He knelt down before me.

"What are you doing? Is it your hip?"

"Rosa?" he said with a laugh.

"What?"

"Will you marry me again?" He pulled out a platinum band with tiny diamonds from his pocket.

"What is that?"

He slipped the ring on my finger. "You haven't answered me."

"I already married you." I smiled at the new ring on my finger.

"Rosa, will you marry me again?"

I smiled at my husband, and the creek sang its tune. "Well, how could I refuse?"

He was a gift from God. After all my years of playing alone as a child, I was rewarded with a playmate who would love me through every beautiful birth to every sad goodbye. I was crazy about him— even after all these years.

I couldn't wait to tell my sister about Manuel giving me such a lovely ring. I wasn't sure whether to wait until I saw her or call her right then and there.

A few days later, we headed to the airport. I was nervous and excited to fly in an airplane. It would be my first time.

Manuel said, "Just so you know … a few more people are coming with us to Mexico."

"Is Lorena all right with having so many people visit? We should let her know so that we can have some of us stay in the hotel."

"Don't worry. I already made reservations," he said.

"So, how long have you been keeping this a secret from me?"

"A while."

"Where did you get the money for this ring ... this fabulous, amazingly beautiful ring?"

"I know how to save money, remember?"

That was true. For every penny earned, there was a penny saved.

"First-class," he said.

The customer service representative at the airport handed us our tickets.

"First-class?" I asked.

"We're traveling in style," he said.

"With what money?"

"Our children gave us a little gift." He handed me my ticket.

Our sons were both smiling and nodding as if they too had been part of this surprise.

"How much did this cost?" I asked.

"Just enough to get us seats where we can spread out and have a dinner for two. I hope they serve steak!"

"We'll have to live on beans and tortillas for the next few weeks," I said.

"Yum," he said.

"Ay, Manuel," I said, allowing myself to enjoy the moment.

I was not a fan of turbulence. Roller coasters were better. At least you could see where you were going. The steak dinner was better than it had been on the train, but I was afraid the turbulence would make me throw up. "Look! They have phones on the plane. I could call my sister."

"Nope, not going to happen." He handed me a magazine.

We arrived late in Tarandacuao. There was nothing but darkness and trees around us. I woke up as the taxi came to a bumpy road outside the ranch where my sister lived. I remembered everything as if it had been two days ago rather than two years ago.

She came out to hug me.

Alejandro took our suitcases inside, and we were greeted with a feast of coffee, tortillas with honey and butter, pan dulce, mangoes, papaya, and pomegranates.

I had never been so hungry in my life. Traveling was exhausting and made me famished. I wasn't sure if I was ready for bed or ready to eat.

Lorena said, "Let me show you to your rooms—and then we'll have something to eat!"

She was a lovely hostess, and I never wanted to let go of her hand.

I washed my face and brushed my hair. The excitement of getting to visit with my sister woke me up again as I splashed water on my face.

"I'm ready," I said, leaving Manuel behind to wash up.

"Come in!" said my sister, finding a place for me at her table. "How have you been?" Her skin was dark and wrinkled, her hair was tied up in a neat, little bun, and her smile was as bright as the sun.

"Very well," I said.

"You look so pretty." Lorena touched my cheek and played with my gray curls.

"So do you." I took a tortilla, put a little honey on it, rolled it up, and gave it to my sister.

"*Café?*" Without letting me answer, she poured a deep, dark blend into my cup. "Hmmm," she said, noticing my new ring.

"Pretty, isn't it?" I was so excited to show her and embarrassed at the same time for having such extravagant jewelry.

She smiled. "When did he give it to you?"

"The other day in California." My ring sparkled in the dim light.

"He's a lucky guy," she said.

All of the adults came into the kitchen and feasted on the midnight snack. My sons made everyone laugh with their ridiculous stories of hiking in the Redwood Forest.

"And then Manuelito comes out of from behind a tree with a sheet over himself and trips over some vine, scaring all of the kids who were told stories about La Llorona."

After a few hours, Manuel said, "The sun is about to come up."

"We should let you get some rest." Lorena got up to gather the dishes from the table.

"I think we'll sleep late tomorrow," I said.

"It is tomorrow," Manuel said.

Everyone went to sleep, and as soon as I began nodding off, I was brought back to reality by the loudest cock-a-doodle-doo right outside our window.

We were definitely on a ranch.

When I fell asleep, I dreamed about the chickens and pigs on my parent's farm, the barn where Manuel and I rehearsed our plays, and Mama and Papa and their love for each other.

In the morning, I called Mama to tell her we had arrived safely and told her I wished we could have brought her with us again, but she decided that it was best that she stayed behind. I knew she was safe, but I thought of her often. My grandson was watching her.

"Is she all right?" I asked.

"Yes, Abuelita. She's watching her soap operas and eating soup. She loves watching the kids. Don't worry! Have a great time!"

"Let me say goodbye to her. Mama, I love you—and we will be coming home soon. I'll call you tomorrow. May God bless you."

Mama said, "Blessings to you, my daughter. I love you very much."

I hung up the phone, hoping I hadn't spent too much money on the call.

Lorena said, "Don't worry! I never call anyone. Why don't we go to the Ojo de Dios and have a swim?"

"I didn't bring a bathing suit," I said.

"You think I wear a bathing suit? I'm sixty-eight. We're just going to wet our feet." She led the way.

We were gone the whole day, hiking through the trees and playing in the water with my grandchildren. It was nighttime. I had hoped to take a walk around the ranch and visit my parent's gravesite, but it would have to wait until tomorrow.

Lorena led me to my room. "Better get some sleep."

"Where's Manuel?" I asked.

"Oh, they should be back soon … probably at the cantina."

"The cantina?" I was not comfortable with my husband going out drinking with Alejandro and my sons without me.

"Don't worry. They should be back soon. You worry too much." She kissed my cheek and left me alone in my room.

Something's up, I thought.

Two hours later, I heard a jeep outside the house and ran to the window to see if they were going to be stumbling in after too much tequila. He had never been a drinker.

I jumped back into bed, and when I heard Manuel's footsteps, I pretended to sleep. "Where were you?" I asked when he got into bed.

"Oh, sorry. I didn't mean to wake you. Go back to sleep," he said.

"Were you with Alejandro?"

"Yes, we had dinner and then came home," he said quickly.

"Why didn't you invite us?"

"Well, you were visiting with your sister, and we thought we would let you have a day together and get some dinner."

"I wish you had come with us. The water was beautiful," I said.

"My love, I was just having some dinner with Alejandro."

"I'm just saying, you were so romantic the other day, and today it's like you'd rather be with Alejandro."

"The truth is, we went to the airport to pick up some people," he said.

"What people?"

"Well, it was supposed to be a surprise, but as you can see, it cannot be," he said.

"What people?"

"Well, Enrique and Manuelito thought it would be great if the other children could be here with us—like for a family reunion of sorts!"

I got out of bed, put on my robe and slippers, and walked out to the kitchen.

My children were sitting around the table and eating another midnight feast.

"*Mis bebes!*" I hugged each one at a time. I was so thankful to see their beautiful faces. Viola, Olivia, Katarina, Desdemona, and Juliet were all here with us in Mexico. My heart was beating faster than ever, and I was laughing so hard that tears were coming out of the corners of my eyes. Some of them had never met my sister before, and it was amazing to have us all together in one room.

My sister served more coffee, and I passed around the basket of tortillas.

I wanted to stay up all night, but everyone kept saying they were tired and had to go to bed.

"But we're on vacation. There's no reason to go to bed early," I said.

"I'm tired," my sister said.

"Oh, then we should go to bed," I said.

"Good night everyone!" Manuel said.

"*Buenas noches, hijos!*" I said as my children went off to sleep.

I said, "Can you believe we are all here at the same time?"

Manuel said, "We sure are!"

"I don't remember the last time we were all together like this."

"You should get some sleep," he said.

"How can you sleep? All of your children are here together with us in Mexico—at my sister's ranch." I wished I could go kiss each of their faces.

Manuel began snoring, and I eventually fell asleep in his arms.

I woke up to the aroma of coffee coming from the kitchen, and as the sky turned orange, I got up and dressed for breakfast. I went straight to the kitchen and began making tortillas.

Lorena walked into the kitchen with a tray of eggs and fruit. "*Buenos dias, hermana!*"

I noticed that Manuel had also gotten up earlier than me and was nowhere to be found. "How early did you get up?"

"You know, I'm so old that I hardly sleep anymore," she said as she ate a piece of mango.

"Mmm," I said, taking a piece for myself.

"Stay here." She left the room for a moment and returned with a large round box.

"What's this?" I opened the box and removed the tissue paper that covered white satin and lace with tons of beautiful embroidery.

"Today is your wedding day … again, and this time, I get to be your madrina!"

"Wedding day?"

She seemed so happy with herself for having kept this secret for so long.

"I didn't think we would actually have a wedding! I just thought he gave me a ring for our anniversary! I never thought ..." I looked out the window and saw the grand oak tree on the hill covered in white streamers and guests waiting for me to join them.

"Let's get you ready." She pulled out a cream-colored dress with lovely lace and beading.

"This lace is so delicate," I said.

"It came from Mama's dress," she said.

I immediately started to cry. I was overwhelmed by the moment.

"Why are you crying? This is a happy day. I didn't get to see you get married the first time. Now dry your eyes—and let's get ready."

My sister helped me with my dress and hair and then put some lipstick on my lips. She also wore a lovely dress and held a bouquet of roses from her garden. "Here is your bouquet. The boys are waiting for us outside."

My sons came by horse and wagon and took me to the top of the hill where my mother and father's graves rested. They would be at my wedding too.

Musicians were playing "Ave Maria" while my grandson sang, and I walked with my five daughters behind me and my sister by my side.

Among all the flowers, white streamers, and people, Manuel was the brightest light on that hill.

As I took his hand, the sun began to glow around us. I was a young bride again.

The wedding was a successful surprise. Manuel and Alejandro had been planning for weeks. As I held my sister's hand and watched everyone dancing at the reception, I realized something. "You have five girls and two boys like me," I said.

We watched our husbands dancing with our daughters.

"And I married a man much like your husband," said Lorena. "I thought the same thing."

"Does he ever tell you not to worry?" I asked.

"All the time," she said.

"We were lucky to find them."

"And we were lucky to find each other." My sister kissed me on the forehead.

That night, as I lay next to my husband, I couldn't stop talking. "Wasn't it lovely how my sister toasted us and danced with Alejandro? And the girls! Weren't they just lovely in their dresses! Wake up, Manuel! How can you sleep on our wedding night!" I pushed him lightly on the shoulder.

"Come here," he said, bringing me closer.

"What did you love the most about today?" I asked as I settled into his arms.

"So many things," he said sleepily.

"Was it the food?" I asked, remembering the delicious barbecue and my sister's tortillas.

"The food was good. I liked the *mole*," he said.

"Did you like the music?" I asked.

"I liked the music," he said.

"The *champagne*?" I asked.

"It made me sleepy," he said.

"You mean drunk," I said with a laugh.

"I'm not drunk, my love. I'm just tired. I'm sure we have a long day of more celebrating tomorrow."

"But what did you love the most? What was your favorite part?"

I heard him exhale, as if he'd fallen asleep.

I was too excited to sleep, but I let him rest. After everything he had done for me—every sweet glance and gentle gesture throughout our whole lives together—he deserved it.

He whispered, "This is what I love." And he held me in his beautiful, ever-loving arms.

Printed in the United States
By Bookmasters